THE TOWN THAT WOUDN'T DIE

2o
Enjoy the read Lynn
Luick

LYNN LUICK

Angel Without Wings

Silver Buck and the Apaches

A Second Chance To Live

Silver Buck Undercover

Silver Buck - First Book of Silver Buck Series

Iron Blood

BOOKSIDE Press

BookSide Press
877-741-8091
www.booksidepress.com
orders@booksidepress.com

CONTENTS

1

My horse Red and me were walking down the dusty trail. I named him Red cause that was the first name that came to me at the time. The sun was straight up and it felt like it was burning a hole in my black hat. It was mid-August, but Red still didn't say anything.

He's the only company I've had since the Captain sent me to check on some goings on out here in West Texas. My badge is in my pocket where I keep it until I find out the layout in the town or area I'm heading. The Texas Ranger's badge sometimes attracts lead in some of the places I'm been and that could be downright painful if you know what I mean. My water and food ran out yesterday, that's why I'm walking beside instead of on Red's back. He hadn't had any water or food either. For miles all that could be seen was cactus and sagebrush or the like. The last water hole we came to looked to be dried up a month or so ago.

As I looked ahead I could see what looked to be a town. But I couldn't be sure it was sort of hazy or maybe it was my brain frying. We kept going until the heat was just unbearable. I stumbled and fell and the last thing I seem to remember was my head hitting a rock sticking up out of the desert sand.

When I came to instead of the sun being in my eyes I was in the shade looking up at the underside of a roof. I was lying on a porch of some kind of building. As I reached to my head where it seemed to hurt my hand came away with blood all over it. My hat was on the porch beside me not on my head. I remember it falling off as I hit the ground. Red was standing at the hitching rail with his reins in the dust of the street and there was a full water trough that Red was drinking out of. I couldn't seem to get Red to tell me what happened, I just knew he had seen everything.

How I came to be here I couldn't say, but it is sure I didn't fill up my canteen and put myself on this porch. As I made it to my feet on my weak legs and walked over to the water trough I soaked my bandana and put it to my head where the blood came from. I could tell the cut on my head had been cleaned before, the blood was fresh and no dried blood around the wound. The water felt cool and refreshing to my pounding head and there was a knot where the cut was but it wasn't too bad. As more of my senses came back I looked around and saw that nobody seemed to be around and there were some tumbleweeds blowing down the street. Knocked out like that I could now have been dead. I reached down and pulled my .45 out of my holster and checked it for dirt and dust but it was clean as a whistle. I walked Red toward the stable after I picked up my hat and put it where it belonged on my aching head. The sun was getting low in the west as I opened the stable door and walked in. I yelled for someone but there was no answer. This was very strange the inside was neat and there was hay in the stalls and in the loft. Taking the saddle off Red I took some hay and rubbed him down. Then went to the storeroom and sure enough there were oats in a grain sack with a stoop. I fed him some oats and took my rifle and saddle-bags and left for the hotel.

As I walked down the street the puzzle grew. The tumbleweeds were now gone and the streets were clean and the buildings seemed to be intact. No windows were broke. I looked in the bank, saloon, and general store but as I walked into the hotel I still had seen no people or animals anywhere and the stores seemed to be clean and ready for business.

Inside the hotel it was the same no people and very clean. Even all the keys to the rooms were on all the pegs where they belonged when the rooms were empty. I rang the little silver bell, which was shiny thinking no one would show. No one did so I took key number 9 off the pegboard and started walking up the stairs. I noticed board number 11 creaked going up the stairs but I was too tired to care and went on up to my room. As I turned the key, all this is very funny, it turned so easy that I could swear someone oiled it not so long ago. There was no sign of rust anywhere on the doorknob. Even in some of the best hotels in Dallas you could find rust somewhere and this sure wasn't Dallas.

As I opened the door I was bewildered again. There was a clean curtain on the window and it wasn't torn anywhere and there was clean sheets on the bed and there was no sign of dirt or dust anywhere in the room even with a wide-open window. By all normal logic with no people in town and the window open there had to be dust and dirt and some rain spots, for it had bound too rain the last few months. But right now I was to worn out and my head still hurt so I really didn't care. I laid down on the perfectly made bed and was off in a dream world of my own.

I woke up in the morning with the sun already well up in the sky and I was hungry as a bear after a long winter sleep. As I started to my feet I noticed my boots were off. I know they were on when I laid down last night. I just sat there thinking what is going on here. It was like putting together a puzzle with a piece missing. One thing is for sure someone has to be in this town besides me.

I got my boots back on and started toward the stairs. As I rounded the corner to the stairs, I know I saw a shadow, toward the lobby and hurried down but no one seemed to be there. Now I noticed that step number 11 didn't creak. Someone had fixed it while I had been asleep. As I left the hotel and into the bright sunshine the day was already hot and sizzling and the dust rose and coated my boots as I walked across the street to the diner. As I stepped onto the porch of the diner there was a good fifteen-degree difference from the sun to the shade. I opened the door and a bell sounded as I entered, ting, ting-a-ling.

Believe it or not there was a large steaming plate of bacon and eggs with johnnie-cakes on the table next to the cup of steaming coffee. I sat down and thought, this person wouldn't try to poison me; they saved me from the desert and took my boots off to make me more comfortable, why would they kill me now. So I went ahead and ate and hoped to be right. Anyway I was to hungry to care right now. Well, I was on my way to the stable and wasn't dead yet, so I guess the food was all right.

As I walked down the boardwalk the thought came to me, if my name wasn't Jim Beddly, I would say this wasn't happening. It wasn't like me to feel so unsure of myself. At six foot two inches tall and broad in the shoulders and quick as the next man with a gun this is a very unusual feeling that I hadn't felt since I was eight years old and got caught stealing apples off old Mr. Tanner's trees. Ma really tanned my hide for that one. I never stole anything again. I laughed to myself.

As I made my way to the stable I just had to look into every store again and it was the same clean and neat as before. It was like people were working and living here. As I walked in the stable to check on Red, he had already been fed and watered and I swear someone had rubbed him down with the brush that was laying in the stall now that wasn't there before. Somehow I had to get to the bottom of this.

As I was standing there rubbing Red's neck I heard a noise behind me. I turned around and nothing was to be seen. I rushed to the back door of the barn and looked right and left but nothing was there. This is truly the town that wouldn't die.

I needed to leave but this town seemed to draw me and wouldn't let me go. It was my mind that wouldn't let me leave I realized. I needed to know what and why all these things were happening. My business I was supposed to look into was in a town called Alpine but

Cap said that someone would contact me somewhere near Marfa now a ghost town twenty-six or so miles away from Alpine. Seems the railroad had turned toward Alpine and not through Marfa and everyone moved to Alpine or so was thought. I didn't know how far I had been brought out of the desert. This could be the town; I just didn't know.

There had to be someone doing this. I made up my mind to find out how this person was doing all this without being seen. They had been helping me since I was brought here so I decided to set up a place in the hotel tonight on the first floor and wait until something happened. By not moving around this person would sometime come looking for me instead of me looking for them. I knew they would come looking for me if I didn't even go to feed Red. I knew he would be all right cause this person would feed him.

I wasn't going to light any lanterns or start a fire to cook. I was going to camp outside the kitchen near the dining room in the hotel and wait. Far as I knew the hotel was the only one stocked with food in this town. When I ate in the diner I had checked the kitchen and no food was there so they must had figured I would go there to find food and took it from the hotel's kitchen. I figured they would come in to eat sometime. Soon I hoped. I waited and waited it would soon be dark. I could see the shadows get longer in the street as the sun started to disappear in the west. It was hot in here from the sun beating down on the tin roof all day and no air was moving around. The sweat was starting to run down my face as the day turned to night. Now two hours later it was so dark I couldn't see my hand in front of my face. I just hoped that when they came it would be with a lantern so I could see them. I had to keep taking my hat off to wipe the sweat off my forehead with my bandana. The sweat was burning my half closed head wound and it still hurt when I wiped it. Another two hours went by and I could see through the front door that the half-moon was rising in the eastern sky. I was beginning to think I was wrong and they wouldn't show. Maybe they had food where they lived if that was even in town. I didn't know even that much about this person but I was determined to wait them out as long as it took. I could see a little better now with the moon out and it was a little cooler now with the sun down for the last four hours. It was so quiet that I could hear the tin roof pop with the oncoming of the coolness of the night. It was now that a sound came to my ears. A slight sound but it was different than the normal sounds of the night so I turned my full attention to the sound and I could tell that it was coming my way. I got down behind the bar that was outside the door of the kitchen as far to the floor as my large frame would let me. It wasn't too much longer cause I could see a light coming around the corner about twenty feet from me. I didn't really want to scare them for they had helped me since I was brought to this town and they had probably saved my life out on that hot dessert but I didn't see any way I could help it.

The light was now within five feet of me and as the silhouette passed by me I could see them holding a lantern in their right hand and they had long hair hanging out from under some kind of helmet. Now I could tell it was some kind of mining helmet. What would a girl be doing in this ghost town with a mining helmet on! I was about to find out right now. As I reached out and took hold of her left arm she yelled.

"Please let me go I haven't done anything to you mister."

"I know you all but saved my life. But I didn't know any other way to talk to you. You wouldn't show yourself. I won't hurt you I just want to find out what's going on around here and who you are."

"Well, then let go of my arm you're hurting it."

"I'll let go if you won't run and talk to me and what's your name anyway. It's been a real puzzle."

"Let go and I won't run, I promise. I just didn't know if I could trust you until now. If you were going to kill me you could have already done it."

I let loose of my grip on her and she looked me straight in the eyes and said.

"Before I tell you anything you tell me who you are and what you doing in this town."

"You mean ghost town don't you?"

"You didn't answer my question and this ain't no ghost town. My grandfather found this place. There wasn't nothing here until he showed up."

"Tell me more."

"Nothing doing, you answer my question."

"Sense there seems to be only the two of us here I guess it won't hurt. I was heading to a place called Marfa when I hit my head on a rock. My Captain sent me to investigate some wrongdoings going on in Alpine. The Cap didn't know anything else except I was supposed to meet this person in Marfa. The person didn't sign their name to the letter. Cap sensed some kind of trouble so here I am ready to listen and see if I can help. My name is Jim Beddly and I'm a Texas Ranger."

"Where's your badge?"

"Here in my pocket I usually don't wear it until I see what's going on in a town. Sometimes it can be dangerous to show it to soon. If I hadn't hit my head you wouldn't even know that I was here."

I pulled my badge from my pants pocket and pinned it on my blue shirt pocket. "I'll take it off when I go into Alpine."

"I saw you when you fell and hit your head. That's why you're alive right now. You sound like you're on the level. No one could know I sent that letter to Captain Turbrough but another Ranger. I made sure of that I don't trust anyone in Alpine I rode all the way to El Paso to mail it."

We got up and sat down at a table in the dining room and she turned the lantern up all the way to brighten the room. She took off the mining helmet and I could see that she had pretty blond hair and looked to be about twenty-five or so. I'm not much of a judge of women and their age.

"Now please tell me your name and what's going on so I can try to help you."

"My name is June Grayson and my grandfather was Guy Grayson and he knew John Turbrough, your captain, many years ago before I was born over in East Texas. He told me that he was a Texas Ranger and was going to write him for help. Before he could write him my grandfather was killed by someone in Alpine."

"Why would someone want to kill your grandfather?"

"When the railroad went through Alpine instead of here and people started to move, Gramps tried to tell them about the gold he had found so they would stay but they didn't believe him. Someone did believe him. They beat him up very bad but I guess he didn't tell. He died a few days later."

That's when she started crying and put her head down on the table. But she raised up her head and wiped her eyes and continued.

"He showed me where it was when I was little and that is how I can keep living here. That's why I hide when someone comes to town I think they will try to make me tell where it is."

"That's why the mining helmet."

"Yes, I was out there all day. I have to make sure I'm not being followed when I go. I don't even know if they know I'm here but they know someone buried Gramps. I just want to find who killed him and live in peace."

"Do you have any idea who could have killed him? Just a place to start looking."

"The only one that comes to mind is Ted Abbot that owns the saloon. Far as I know he's the only one that has the money to hire men to do the dirty work and when Gramps was talking about the gold he was one that listen the most."

"No one else, come to mind?"

"There are two rancher that have land over on the other side of Alpine. Tom Davis has a large cattle ranch but it takes so much land to raise one cow that I really don't know how he can make ends meet. He must have over fifty thousand acres out north of town. Then there is Gary Thomas out to the east of town. He's a sheep rancher and him and Davis don't get along at all. He must have twenty thousand acres and I think he does a little better than Davis. Sheep do better on this rocky soil around here. When those two come to town at the same time Sheriff Brady has to sometimes keep them apart. That's all I can think of but they all use to live in Marfa and know about gramps talking about finding a gold mine."

"Well, that's a place to start. If you do talk to anyone or come into Alpine don't tell anyone who I am or what I'm doing here. I won't show my badge until I investigate a while. I'll try to let you know what's going on but I'm going to try to get hired on at one of the ranches so I might not be able to get away often. I'll head to Alpine in the morning after I eat some of your good breakfast."

"Oh, Mr. Beddly; Why you go and say that now?"

"Cause it's the truth. I've been eating my own cooking too long. I'll go up to my room now. I'll see you in the morning. Good-night June and you can call me Jim I'm not too much older than you."

"Good-night Jim. I'll have that hot breakfast ready for you."

I went to my room and turned in thinking about what I was going to do. This might be a tough case. I'll find out more when I hit town and I won't even tell the sheriff who I am. That's how I operate my cases. Before I knew it my eyes were open and I could see the sun rising up over the roof of the building across the street. I gathered up my things and headed down to eat and get Red saddled and head to Alpine. I ate and said bye to June and rode out of the town that still had life in it for now.

This was a lonely place out here where nothing lived without water but cactus and a few mountain goats and desert animals but if there was really gold in these mountains around here as June said it might give someone a reason to kill and try to take over this whole country. I felt good after a few nights rest and good food with a bed to sleep on and the way Red was acting I knew he was mended from that long trek across the desert. I spurred Red into a full gallop and he didn't seem to mind and moved even faster across the miles into Alpine. This was the way my life had been for the last ten years. At my old age of thirty I had seen my share of trouble none of my doing but I seemed to be there to put a stop to it or find who had caused it. This time was different; this was a case of murder, which means that whoever did it will go to any length to have their way around here. I need to put a stop to any more crimes of any kind or murders took place. June acted like she knew what she wanted and was determined to keep her grandfather's dream alive and bring that ghost town back to life. The short time that I had spent with her I was determined to help her with that dream. No matter how I felt it was my job to help good people in this country keep what they had.

This night I spent out under the stars once more on the desert floor eating my own cooking with Red staked out on a small patch of grass I had come upon near a small creek. June had been good enough to pack me some grub for the trail. Tomorrow I would be in Alpine to begin my work. I would have to be very careful and not make too many enemies. I would need all the friends I could roundup if this case was going to be successful and find a way to let June know what was going on. This would all come with the passing of time. I rolled out my bedroll and was asleep out in the nice fresh air.

I woke up just as dawn was breaking and as I heard Red I rolled over and was looking into the barrel of a 44-40 rifle.

"Thanks Red for that warning. Take it easy mister." I threw back my blanket and got up keeping my hands away from my .45 in my holster that I have a habit of sleeping with when out in this wild country.

"What you doing in this country? This is Davis ranch and we don't like strangers coming across this here land."

"I didn't know anyone owned this land. I was just heading into Alpine looking for work."

He lowered the rifle and looked at me.

"You look to be on the level. We have some trouble with cattle rustlers lately. I was told to keep a lookout for any strangers. Get up and get into Alpine before the boss comes along and sees you. It's only ten miles or so away."

"I will, won't even fix breakfast. I'll eat in town, tired of my cooking anyway. I have a little money left from my last job."

"That will be fine mister."

I saddled Red and got in the saddle and headed for town with his eyes on my back all the time.

2

I rode up the street of Alpine about two in the afternoon. I was sure hungry for I didn't want to push my luck by stopping to fix some dinner. I noticed the railroad station to the east end of town with rails going to the northwest and to the east of town. Now I got off Red and tied him to the hitching rail in front of the Long Bar Saloon and that was the biggest sign I've seen since I was in Dallas. They usually have something to eat to draw in men who also drink a lot but I was looking for a little more than eats and drinks. As I pushed the bat winged doors open and walked in all eyes turned to see who had come in. Then they turned back to the bar and kept eaten and drinking. They must have been expecting someone else, I don't know so I walked up to the longest bar I had ever seen in my life and ordered a beer and grabbed a couple of sandwiches and turned and looked around. The bartender put my beer down in back of me and said.

"That a be two-bits stranger."

I put down my two-bits and took a big bite out of the sandwich and a big swig of beer. Then out of the corner of my eye I spotted the range hand that had ordered me off the ranch. He must know a short cut into town to beat me by as much as he did. I had noticed there wasn't any lathered up horse in the bunch outside. I took a chance with my luck and walked over to the table where he was enjoying his drink. He turned and looked up as I approached the table and I thought he was going to choke on the beer he had in his mouth.

"I didn't mean to startle you, I just wanted to let you know there's no hard feeling about this morning. I realize that you were just doing your job."

"In that case have a seat. I sometimes enjoy someone's company besides those mangy old cows."

I said "thanks" as I sat down.

"You seemed to be alright so I was wondering if you would make it to town or just pass us by."

"No, I'm nearly out of money. That's why I'm in here with one beer and two sandwiches. Can't afford the diner. You're the only one I kind of know around here that's why I came over to talk to you."

"I tell you; you must be lucky cause some of the other boys on the ranch might have shot you and then asked what you were doing."

"So that's how it is around here?"

"Well, like I said out there we been having some trouble with cattle missing. I figured I had the drop on you so there wasn't no harm in letting you talk a little."

"I'm glad of that, old Red woke me up to late, he must be as tired of the trail as I am. Like I said I'm not looking for any trouble just a job and if I like it I might just stick around here awhile. You know anyone might be hiring. Done about anything that needs doing around a ranch that you can think of."

"I don't know, some of these boys in here work for Mr. Davis same as I do. They'll be wondering why you picked me to talk to."

Just then two of the men from the bar walked over and pulled up chairs and sat. One of them started in.

"Dean, who is this gent you jawing with, you look like you know each other."

I said, "No we don't know each other just saw him sitting by his self and thought I give him some company to talk to."

"I wasn't talking to you mister."

"Like he said he just walked up and he wanted to know if there was any jobs around, I don't even know his name."

"What's your name mister?"

"Jim Beddly."

"Well Beddly, I'm the foreman at the Davis ranch and there ain't no jobs around these parts. If I was you I'd get on your horse and keep heading east plum out of this country."

"Well Mr. Foreman you ain't me and I think I'll look around here awhile and decide for myself if you don't mind."

"You mind my words. Boys let's get back to the ranch there's work to be done."

The two got up and started toward the door and stopped and turned.

"That means you to Dean."

"I'm coming."

Dean whispered, "Don't rile Bart too much, he's mean. Try the Thomas ranch south of town. It's sheep but it's a job."

"Thanks Dean, I'm sure I'll see you later."

This Bart seemed like a bad one with black hair and a long scar across his chin and a frown that seemed to be frozen on his face. His voice was rough like he had sandpaper in his throat. His sureness seemed to be in his size. He was a couple of inches above my 6'2". But size isn't everything.

They went out the door and a man came over in a nice fanny suit and sat.

"I overheard your discussion with Bart. He didn't seem to like you very much."

"From that little talk we had I don't think he likes anyone that much."

He laughed and stuck out his hand and I shook it.

"I'm Ted Abbot and I own this saloon and some other buildings around town."

"Glad to meet someone more friendly. I'm Jim Beddly."

"I heard Dean, he's one of the few good men working for Davis he was right, try Thomas for a job. You know if you want to get under

Bart's skin that will do it. Davis and Thomas are both good men but most of Davis men are downright bad. Thomas men mostly just want to make a living."

"Seems you hear most everything around here."

"That's my business. Information is the way to get ahead in this town. Now I better get back to my books."

"Thanks for the information. Ted, I would like to know how you got that long bar to this town and in this building."

Ted just laughed on his way to his office.

"Remind me later, it's a long story."

I finished my beer and headed south out of town.

The Thomas ranch was about two miles out of town and I had no trouble as I rode right up to the house, which was small but nice and neat. I could see the barn and corral that looked to be in fine shape with a nice looking bunkhouse nearby. A few horses were in the corral and there were a few sheep around the barn. As I got off Red an older woman came out on the porch with a young girl about thirteen beside her. She was wiping her hands on her apron and shading her eyes against the late afternoon sun.

"May I help you young man."

"Yes ma'am, I'm looking for a Mr. Thomas. I was told in town that he might be hiring and from the smell of what's coming out of the house this must be a fine place to work. I'm Jim Beddly ma'am."

"Thank you for that complement. My husband will be in soon with the men for supper that I was just about done with. You can wait up here on the porch if you want. I better get back to my stove."

"Yes ma'am I'll just wait here for him."

"Sara, you stay out here and keep Mr. Beddly company. You hear."

"Yes ma. Where you from mister?"

"Why all around but I just came from El Paso out west of here."

"El Paso, really I sure would like to see the big city. All I get to see is little old Alpine. Not much to see but school and church on Sunday. The same old building the school is in all week."

"Maybe one day you will get to go to El Paso or a bigger city like Denver or Dallas."

"You've been there to?"

"Yes I have Sara. I like the smaller town myself but wait and see."

"Here comes Pa I guess I'll go finish setting the table for supper."

"Good talking to you Sara."

I saw an older man and five others coming in from the southeast where I could see a mountain in the distant. They dismounted and the one next to the older man said.

"What are you doing around here? We don't need any trouble from any cattleman."

"I'm not here to cause any trouble. I was in town looking for a job and a man named Dean said you might be hiring. A man named Bart came up while me and Dean were talking and let it be known that Mr. Davis wasn't hiring in a rough kind of manner."

The older man said. "I'm Gary Thomas and I know Bart and he yelled at you."

"Well a little. But Dean seem nice enough."

"I been trying to get Dean to come to work with us he's not like the others in that bunch. Says he's a cattleman. Gene needs to learn to give a man a chance to talk. Now what can I do for you."

"I'm sorry Mr. Thomas but you know we've had some trouble." Gene said.

"Mr. Thomas I've heard about some of the trouble around here but I'm not looking for any just a job. I've done just about anything that needs doing on a ranch. It can't be much different than cattle just smaller."

He laughed at that and some of the men did to.

"Tell you what stay for supper and we'll talk and I'll let you know."

"That will be great I've been right down hungry for an hour since I smelled your wife's cooking."

"I know what you mean. I think some of these boys stick around just for that."

"By the way I'm Jim Beddly."

As we went in the house he said, "Ma, we have a guess for tonight."

"I already had Sara set another plate down. If you didn't invite him I was. He likes the smell of my cooking."

"And everyone else within a mile of the house. I'm just glad we're not close to town or we would have half the men out here for supper."

Mr. Thomas said a prayer and as we ate I just couldn't imagine these good people murdering anyone but I need to get to know the men. One or more could be bad. Somehow I needed to get to know some of the hands at Tom Davis's ranch and Tom himself. I didn't know how I was going to do that working here but I had to try cause a murderer was here somewhere.

"Where you from Jim?"

"Pa, he just came from El Paso and he's been to Dallas and Denver."

"Sara, I was asking Mr. Beddly. I see you have the women vote around here."

"Sara's right I had a job in El Paso in an office but I didn't like being cooped up all day. I heard about some ranches out this way so I headed out. My horse Red seems to like it out this way to."

"Well, anyone that thinks that much of his horse, I'd say put him in the barn and give him some oats and get your bedroll in the bunkhouse and stay awhile."

"Thank you Mr. Thomas."

"You work for me you can just call me Gary and my wife here is Bonnie."

"Yes sir, I mean Gary. There's just one thing if it's all right. I may have to go to town after work most of the time."

"Got a girl already picked out? Maybe that gal in the Long Bar."

"Gary, don't josh Jim this soon. Jim, you'll learn my husband it a real funny man."

"Oh Bonnie, we have to have some fun in life. Jim, as long as you work hard what you do after work is your business."

"I'll take the job. I just like to get to know people around where I work and in the town. I've never been in these parts."

Bonnie said. "Gary, I'd like to hear about how you know the gal in the Long Bar."

All the men started laughing and then Bonnie and then Gary were laughing.

That was the end of supper and I headed to the barn leading Red. The barn was cool away from the hot summer sun and as I unsaddled Red and grabbed some hay to wipe off the sweat I heard someone come up behind me and as I turned I saw Gene coming in the barn. He walked up to me and stuck out his hand and as we shook he said.

"I'm Gene the foreman. Sorry I was so blunt with you out front but we have had some trouble with that Tom Davis bunch for a time now. I should have givin' you a chance to talk."

"I understand, you know Gene as long as I work here I'll ride for the brand."

"That's good to hear cause Gary and his family are good people. When you're done bring your roll in the bunkhouse and you can meet the rest of the men you'll be working with. I noticed that you wear your gun low like a gunfighter."

"That sounds good I'll be right in and no I'm not a gunfighter. That's just how my dad wore his and I did the same."

As I entered the bunkhouse Gene came over and showed me my bunk and turned to all the men and said to me.

"I'm sure most of the men got your name at supper but you need to know who you're working with."

He took me down the line of four men and I shook hands as Gene told me their names. There was Slim he wasn't slim at all; he was short and had a belly that would rival Santa Clause. Then there was a young man named Bob that looked like he was trying to grow a beard with not much luck. The third man they called Pickin's. After we shook hands I saw why they called him that. He stuck his finger in his nose and then wiped it on his pants. The last man was Joe. Joe was an older man with a scar on his right cheek of his face. Then Gene said,

"Boys you get to know Jim and tomorrow we'll try to educate him about the sheep business. Any questions Jim.

"Just, when's breakfast. Bonnie is sure a fine cook."

All the men laughed and Slim said.

"You know Jim I use to match my name but I just love to eat Bonnie's cooking so be careful how much you eat."

Everyone roared with laughter as they went to their own bunks. I got my bedroll laid out on my new bunk and took my few belonging and put them in the small chest next to my bunk and I leaned my .44-40 rifle against the wall next to the head of my bunk and hung my gun belt on the right bed post that would be next to the right of my head and then my hat on the left bed post. I was just about settled in when Pickin's came over and sat down on his bed that was next to mine. That's the way life goes the new man gets stuck with the odd ball. Then he spoke up.

"You know Jim this is a good outfit to be with. Gary is a good owner and Gene is a good foreman. Just do what they tell you to do and you will be fine. Good-night."

"Thanks, Pickin's see you in the morning."

I woke up with a little nudge from Pickin's. I had gotten real comfortable in this nice bunk. I had slept straight through the night. Gene came over.

"Are you going to be one of those men we have to kick out of bed?"

"No, just that I been sleeping on the trail to long and this soft bed did me in. Give me a few days to get use to it and I'm sure the hard work will get me started and I smell that breakfast that will sure get me going."

"Well, let's get to the table."

We ate and then got mounded and Gene told Slim to get the dogs out. Slim let them out and we were on our way. There were four dogs and they were in the led all the way up into the foothills of the nearby mountains. As we came to the top of the rise there below us was 2,000 or 3,000 sheep and the dogs were among them barking at the sheep to get them up on their feet. It was a wonder to see as the four dogs just about split the herd in half. Gene came over to me.

"See Jim the dogs do most of the work, they love it. Just follow the bunch on the right and just make sure the sheep don't stray. If they do just call out to Breed or Blackie and they will get them back in the bunch. The other two dogs are Toby and Whip. They will be heading to the north and your bunch will be going to the west. The grass will be better in those two new areas. Slim and Pickin's will be with you just ask them if you have any questions. I'll be with the other bunch. The dogs do most of the work and Slim knows where to let them graze."

"Yes boss, I'll do my best. Is this all the sheep?"

"No, we have 5,000 more in different parts of the ranch. That's around 8,000 plus any new lambs that may be born. I better get just talk to Slim and Pickin's they know about everything."

When Gene was gone Pickin's came over and I could see Slim in the lead.

"You all right Jim? It's pretty easy until shearing season that's about a month away."

"What's shearing?" Pickin's yelled out.

"Breed back here." The dog came back and rounded up two sheep that had gotten behind the main bunch. Then he said.

"Shearing is when we get all the sheep together and cut the wool off the sheep and take the wool to the railroad in Alpine for shipping back east to the textile factories to make clothes and the like. That's how Gary gets money to run this place. Tom Davis and his men have attack us and killed lots of our sheep. In a life of a sheep their wool could bring in a few thousand dollars so that is a ton of money that has been killed."

"The sheriff doesn't do anything about it?"

"We never caught them red handed but no one else has a reason to kill the sheep. Davis claims the sheep eat the grass to close to the ground and it doesn't grow back but that's not true. It grows back faster than with the cattle. I've seen both so I know."

"It seems that Davis wouldn't care it's Gary's land. As long as the sheep stay on Gary's ranch."

"You would think so. Slim stopped so we're here."

Slim came over to us and said.

"Let's get back to the ranch."

He yelled for Breed and Blackie to come along. About half way back we met up with the other men and got back to the ranch before supper. That night I headed to Alpine. As I was about to get on Red when Gene came over with Sara.

"How you like it today, Jim?"

"It was good the dogs did most of the hard work. Pickin's said that it was this way until shearing comes."

Sara spoke up. "Yep, that's when even ma and me get to help right over there in that long shed." Then Gene spoke to me,

"There's enough room in that shed to hold all the men and ten sheep at a time. The dogs keep the rest of the sheep bunched up outside and there's also a big room for the wool to be stored until we take it to town. I'll show you before we start the shearing next month."

Sara said, "You going to town?"

"Yea, just want to get to know some of the people around town and get use to the terrain around these parts. I should be back early, today was some tiring and I'm not much of a drinkin' man just a beer or two."

"You better watch for that bunch of Davis men they can raise cane sometimes."

"I'll be careful."

Sara said, "Better watch for those gals in the Long Bar. I heard tell of them."

Just then we heard someone come up behind us. As we turned Gary was standing there.

"Young lady, you've no business talking about those women. Get to the house and help your ma with the dishes."

"Oh, pa I didn't mean any harm."

"Sorry Jim sometimes she hears to much around all these men."

"I better get to town. I'll watch out for Davis's men and the gals."

They were both laughing as I rode out. On my way to town I kept a sharp lookout for the different features around the area. There were a few places where a person could watch the trail and not be seen or be ambushed from and I noticed that there was more than one way to get to town. I will have to explorer the different ways and find some new ways just for safety. Might have to use a different trail every time, it keeps one from being ambushed. As I tied Red in front of the Long Bar I saw Dean's horse. As I went inside I saw Dean sitting with Bart having a drink. I got a beer and walked over to their table.

"May I have a seat?"

"No, you can't, I don't drink with sheep herders."

Dean spoke. "Bart, if it wasn't for you he'd be on our ranch. So leave him alone."

"I'm leaving, you better be careful Dean. You know where you get your bread buttered."

Bart left and I sat down. I notice Bart went over to another table and was talking to a man I hadn't seen before when I was in here.

"He doesn't make friends easy does he?"

"No, he's that way to everyone but Tom over there. He's probably telling him about you being a sheep man and how I seem to be friendly toward you. We all heard you got on with Gary. How you like it?"

"It's a lot less work than with the cattle. The dogs do most of the work. I hope me talking to you don't get you in trouble with Tom cause he seems to be coming this way."

"That's Bart's doing."

"Hello son I'm Tom Davis. I just like to get to know any new men that come to town. Bart was just telling me that you went to work for Gary today. You don't look like a man that worked with sheep before?" As we shook hands I said.

"Good to meet you Mr. Davis. I've never worked with sheep before but as I was just telling Dean here it seems to be easier work than with cattle and Bart told me when I came to town that there wasn't any jobs at your ranch so I headed to Gary's and I just love Bonnie's cooking. I haven't had eats like that since I left home."

"I can understand that but Bart miss spoke and our cook is a fine cook."

I looked Dean's way and he was shaking his head no.

"You offering me a job?"

"Yes, I am."

"Not right now, I'm going to give it a chance at Gary's ranch awhile. But I sure appreciate the offer. I might ride over and look your place over one day off."

Tom left and went back to the table where Bart was. He looked a little mad.

"Jim, you better watch your step Tom's not use to be turned down by anyone."

That's when a saloon girl came over and sat down.

"Who's your friend Dean, he's a new one around here?"

"Lola, this is Jim Beddly, right Jim?"

"That's right and it's a pleasure to meet a lovely girl like you Lola in a place like this."

I waved for the bartender to bring Lola and me another beer.

"Thank you Jim how nice of you. It's good to see a new face in town and a right down handsome one to."

We talked awhile and Lola asked some questions and then left and Dean said.

"Watch that one she does Ted's bidding. He wants to learn more about you and she belongs to him if you know what I mean."

"Well, Dean I'll be sure and be careful. I better get back to the ranch morning comes early around here."

As I left the saloon I turned and saw Lola and Bart go over and sit down at Ted's table and Tom was heading my way as I left the saloon. Tom came over as I got into the saddle.

"I just wanted to ask you to think about coming to work for me. Don't let Bart get under your skin. He gets the job done that I need doing and that's what counts with me."

"You better watch him; you might not be the only one he's working for."

"What you mean by that?"

"Just turn around and see the two he's talking to right now. How many times has Lola cozied up to you and got information from you? Who did she talk to after and the same goes for Bart?"

As I turned Red and headed out of town I saw Tom go to the bat-winged door and look inside and then got on his horse. I took a different trail back to the ranch I wasn't looking to get dead my second night in town. The lights were already out as I came to the barn. As I found my way to my bunk in the dark and sat down to take off my boots I heard Pickin's move.

"You back so early. I thought you might be one of those that stays out all night and sleeps in the saddle all day."

"No just trying to get to know some people around town. See you in the morning."

"Just be careful who you get involved with Gary and his family are good people and we wouldn't want anything to happen to them."

"I already figured that out. Don't worry about that."

The next morning we went to breakfast and Gary said.

"Boy's we're going up to the north range and check on the herd up there. I know it's a far ride and we won't get back tonight, but it has to be done at least once a week. Bonnie fixed up some grub for us so all we have to do is heat it over the campfire. I didn't want you to feel neglected. Gene, if you don't mind we'll let Jim here take Bonnie and Sara to town or we might not eat next week."

"Oh Gary, I didn't let on to no such thing. I just need some things to make my cooking just right."

"Boss, that's alright with me if Jim stays here and take the women folk to town. We sure want Bonnie's cooking to be just right as always."

Everyone was laughing. "Anyway we'll get Jim next time we head out that way."

I went out and hitched up the buckboard and the men and Gary headed out and the women folk and me went to town. I didn't mind cause I needed to try to work things out on the case when Bonnie said.

"Well, Jim do you have a girl back in El Paso."

"No ma'am I'm just a lonely cowboy. Anyway I never found a gal that could put up with me and I'm not in one spot to long." Sara spoke up.

"Jim, I don't find that likely. I think you are such a fine looking man don't you think so ma."

I was smiling and laughing.

"Sara, you don't say things like that in front of Jim it might embarrass him even if it's true."

"Thank you ma'am. You know this is a real fine looking country around here. This could grow in my bones. There's all this flat land and off a ways there's rocky mountains sticking right up towards the sky." Sara said.

"Some say there's gold in some of those mountains but I think pa found his gold in the sheep that he herds."

"You know you could be right some times that a safe and easier way to get your money."

Bonnie spoke up. "If that Mr. Davis would just leave us alone."

"What has he done? Why hasn't the sheriff done anything about it?"

"Well, some of our sheep have turned up missing and one waterhole was poisoned and we lost some sheep before the men found it. Then there are the night raids and some sheep turn up dead."

"Anyone ever seen some of his men doing these things."

"No, and that's why John hasn't done anything. Says he needs proof and we say who else could be doing it. It just don't make any sense to me."

"I've seen this happen before and it turned out to be a third party that was trying to get two people fighting. It may not be that way here but someone will slip up one day."

I left it at that as we rode up to the general store in Alpine. I helped the women down and we went inside. I looked around as the storekeeper came up and was helping Bonnie. There was a tug on my shirt and as I started to turn around a familiar voice said.

"Meet me out back, we'll talk."

3

It was June I recognized her voice. Just like her, as I turned she was already gone. I went out back and there she was hiding behind a rain barrel.

"Come on out here June we can talk."

"I didn't think we should be seen together."

"It's alright, I'll just say you're a girl I met on the trail."

"You find out anything yet."

"Some but there is a lot more behind this. I'm working for Thomas and they seem to be nice folks. I've met Davis but haven't got to know him yet. His foreman Bert seems bad and may have something going on with Abbot and the girl Lola. It's only been a week this is going to take some time. If you can come in and meet me here every two weeks or so I may have more."

"There was two men out my way this week but they didn't see me. I'm afraid every time I go and come from the mine that someone will follow me."

"What did they look like?"

"Well, let's see, one had a scar on his chin and was a big man with black hair, kind of unkempt. The other just was of average size with brown hair with a bare spot on back of his head below the hat line and had a little limp like he'd been thrown off a horse and stoved up his leg."

"I know one and I'll keep a lookout for the other. If they come back see if they meet someone, I better get back now. I'll see you in a few weeks be careful."

I headed back inside and met up with Bonnie and Sara. They were just about done so I started to load the supplies in the wagon. Bonnie and Sara were standing on the walk in front of the store as I was about to throw the last 50lb. sack of flour in the back of the wagon when I heard Sara yell for me to watch out. As I turned I ducted and there was a fist about to hit me flush in the face but Sara had yelled just in time so Bart's fist went right over my head. He staggered cause of the missed blow but my right caught him right in his big belly and his mouth flew open trying to get some wind and my left foot caught his right boot and he fell in the dirt on his face. He was up on his feet in a flash but my left was ready for him and landed right under his chin and he was again in the dirt on his back. This time he didn't move so I threw the sack of flour in the wagon and helped Bonnie and Sara in the wagon and jumped up on the seat and we headed out of town toward the ranch. Sara said.

"That was some fight."

"Sara, you know better."

"Sorry ma, but it was wasn't it Jim?"

"I didn't notice any fight, just some mangy critter got in the way."

We all laughed as we headed down the road home. When we got to the ranch I unloaded the wagon and then headed to the barn as the boys came in from the range. An hour later we were all up to the house for dinner.

"Jim, Bonnie told me what happen in town."

"It was nothing boss Bart just couldn't seem to stay out of the dirt."

Everyone laughed cause they had already heard the story from Sara.

"Well, you be careful tonight when y'all boy's go to town, Bart won't forget that."

As we were riding to town I told them.

"Thought you boys were going to stay out overnight? Listen boys if Bart starts for me just let me handle him. Just keep his men out of it. No since in any one else getting hurt." Gene said. "You know Jim we were going to be out till tomorrow but the boss thought we better come back in with the trouble we been havin'. You boys know, I sure would have gave anything to see old Bart face down in the dirt."

We were all laughing as we tied up in front of the Long Bar and walked through the bat-wings and headed to the bar. I saw Bart over in the corner talking to Ted Abbot and then I spotted Dean at one of the tables and took my beer over and sat down. Pickin's and Gene came along with me.

"What's going on Dean? Haven't seen you around."

"Just been at the line shack for a while over by y'all's place. But I heard what happen today and Bart's fit to be tied."

"Well, he asked for it."

From across the room Bart yelled.

"Dean, you better get away from those sheep-headers."

"I'll talk to who I want to when I'm not workin'."

"Ever since that one came to town you sure have changed and became friendly to the likes of them."

"Maybe I don't like the way you run things out at the ranch. Remember I spent two nights at the line shack this week."

"You better shut that mouth of yours and you better get your things tonight and head out. We don't need your kind around anymore."

"Fine, I'll head out tonight."

"You know what you're doing Dean."

"I'm tired of that loud mouth of his."

"Gene, Gary's been trying to get me to come to work and I'm ready."

"Well Dean I would say yes, I like you, but you know Gary he does the hiring. Why don't you get your things and stay in the bunkhouse tonight and you can talk to Gary in the morning at breakfast."

"Thanks Gene I'll do it."

I said, "I'll go out with you Dean, I don't trust Bart. He looked mad when you mention the line shack. What happened out there?"

"Can't say right now."

Dean and me got up to leave after we finished our beer.

"Wait a minute big man I not be done with you."

"Why you talking to me Bart or do you want another dirt bath."

I could see the mad in his eyes as his hand found the butt of his gun but mine was already out and pointing right at Bart's face.

"I wouldn't do that if I was you. I wouldn't want to blow off that pretty face of yours."

Everyone was laughing, even Bart's own men, as he stormed out of the Long Bar. They were still laughing as we heard Bart's horse's hooves on the hard packed ground in the street leaving town. That's when Ted Abbot came over.

"You two better be careful tonight. I know that one and I never seen Bart take that from anyone before. He's not one to care if he kills you from the front or back."

"Come on Dean we'll go get your gear. Gene you and Pickin's want to come with us."

"I think we'll have a couple more beers right Pickin's."

"Sure thing boss. Y'all two just watch that darkness out there."

As we turned to go I noticed a man that was talking to Ted leave and he had a slight limp in his left foot. As he went out the door he pulled down his hat, I guess from the bright sun but there was no sun tonight, and there was a bald spot on the back of his head.

"Who's that Dean going out the door?"

"That's Shorty. We call him that cause one leg is a little shorter than the other. He hangs with Bart most of the time."

We headed down the dusty street of Alpine heading to Tom Davis cattle ranch.

It was a very dark night; the moon hadn't shown its face as of yet.

"I sure wish that moon would rise this ain't a good night to be headin' down a dark road with Bart mad as a wet hen."

"I sure never seen Bart so mad as when he looked into the barrel of your gun back there."

"We better keep our eyes peeled and our guns handy."

"Jim, lets head off the trail this way, it's a short cut I know. Bart may be watching for us on the main trail. This will take us around to the back of the bunkhouse."

"Dean what was this about when you were out at the line shack?"

"Well I shouldn't say anything until I know if Gary will hire me."

"You know when something is wrong it's wrong no matter who you work for."

"I know you're right but let's wait till I get my gear and we're out of here. I had to open my mouth back there. Now Bart will sure be after both of us."

We rode down the back trail to the Davis ranch. There was plenty of mesquite brush and scrub oak on this trail.

"I hope this mesquite don't tear up the horses. Why would anyone use this way?"

"Just stay behind me and we'll make it alright. That's why I use it sometimes cause no one else does and not at night for sure. Tom keeps it like this to ward off attacks from this way. My horse knows the way even in the dark I come this way often. Sometimes it keeps from getting a hole in the back."

We rode along in silent for a while then all a sudden we were out of the brush and I could see a light in the short distant. It was about ten minutes when we rode up in front of the bunkhouse. As we dismounted Tom was coming down from the house. Dean was in and out of the bunkhouse in a matter of minutes. He was tying his gear in back of his saddle when Tom reached us.

"Dean, what you doing coming in from the back way and what is this sheepherder doing with you."

"Bart fired me in town and Jim here came with me to get my gear. I'm staying at Gary's ranch tonight."

"So you're going over to their side. So much for loyalty."

"Boss, I like you but as long as you have Bart as your ramrod I'll just stay away."

"What do you mean? What did Bart do? He was just here and got Jess and Art and left in a hurry back toward town."

"You just better watch your stock I know Gary and his men aren't stealing your cattle. It's someone closer to you."

"Are you saying Bart has something to do with it?"

As we mounted Dean said, "Just watch your back I wouldn't want to see a hole in it. If I said he was, you wouldn't believe me and if I was you I wouldn't trust any of the others either."

I said, "Tom I know you might not trust me but I would investigate what Dean said without confronting Bart. If you need some help I'll be around."

"That goes for me to Tom."

We headed on the road to Gary's ranch. The moon was now coming up in the eastern sky, which was full of stars, and the road was bright and clear.

"What you said back there do you really believe it? Do you have proof?"

"Not really, just when I was at the line shack I heard some movement one night and I went outside a ways and I saw three riders and they didn't seem to be out for a pleasure ride. They were herding about fifty head of cattle. That's all I know except I heard a little jiggle like I have heard Bart's spurs make some times. I just went back to bed but the more I worried on it I thought what would men be movin' cattle at night for."

Before I could get out another question a shot rang out from the west in the still of the night. We both were out of our saddles and in the brush along the side of the road in a split second with our rifles in our hands and our horses close behind. Then another shot came from the east then the south. We seemed to be surrounded but we knew they couldn't get a good shot at us. They were just shooting in the dark either to scare us or hoping to hit us. Then a rough voice spoke up out of the dark.

"You two better hit the trail out of this county and don't look back. Next time we won't miss."

We stayed in our hole for a while and not another shot came at us so we mounted and hurried on to the ranch.

"Dean, did you recognized that voice?"

"No, I didn't. I know it wasn't Bart's. If I heard it again I will."

"I know I will to."

We rode into the yard of Gary's bunkhouse and got our horses in the barn and were inside and in bed and I was asleep as my head hit the pillow. When I woke there was Pickin's staring at me and then at Dean.

"What is it Pickin's?"

"What's Dean doing here?"

Dean looked up rubbing his head and yawing.

"Pickin's I got fired last night and Gene said I could stay and talk to Mr. Thomas this morning for a job. Don't you remember. You were there."

"Well yea, alright then but you two better get up or you'll miss breakfast." He said as he stuck his finger in his nose.

As Dean and me was walking to the house Gary met us coming from the barn.

"I hear tell that you might want to put your feet under our table from now on. You finally tried of those cattle."

"Yes sir I sure would like to stay here but it's not the cattle, it's the men that run with the cattle."

"Well, I'm glad to have you for any reason we better get to breakfast before ma gives it to the hogs. Then we'll head out."

"Yes sir."

As we ate everyone was quiet except for Sara.

"Jim, I thank you."

"For what Sara?"

"For bringing Dean in with you last night. I always thought he should be working with us."

Dean spoke up. "Thank you Sara, I'm glad to be here and this food is great Mrs. Thomas over at the Davis ranch we just had an old cookie that his best meal was beans and more beans but I see some of the others might disagree with you Sara. Look fellows I just like cattle and I liked Mr. Davis but I just got my belly full of Bart. I know y'all are good folks and I hope you will learn that I'm here to help and not cause trouble."

Gary said, "I'm sure the boys will give you the benefit of the doubt right boys."

Then Pickin' said. "I know all these months we been having trouble Dean you never had a hand in it."

Slim, Bob and Joe were shaking their heads yes, that was a true fact.

Here Bonnie said, "You know Dean around here everyone calls me Bonnie."

"That's fine Bonnie and this is the best cooking I've eatin' since I left home. My mother was a fine cook."

"See boys anyone that talks about their mother like that ain't at all bad."

Everyone had a great laugh and then we all headed out to the range. Gary told Dean to go with Pickin's and me along with two of the dogs Breed and Blackie. Dean picked up on the work right away and saw that the dogs did most of the work.

"With those dogs what are we here for?"

Pickin's said. "They do a lot but when we bring the sheep from the high country it takes everyone to handle the flock and then there is shearing season that will wear you out for about two weeks. You see how wooly the sheep are well in about a month we will be sheering them and sending the wool to market. It will take you a good while to learn to sheer."

Pickin's headed off to the other side of the herd. Then Dean asked me.

"Last night you didn't say anything about who shot at us and why."

"I been running that around in my mind. I don't know everyone around here but I think someone is making trouble to try to get a hold of these two ranches and I don't think Gary or Tom knows anything about what's going on. Let me know if you hear that voice again."

"I still can't place that voice but it will hit me one day. Why do you want to know?"

"One day I'll tell you all about it. I hear you talk and I think you might be suited for another kind of job."

The end of the day came and we were all in the bunkhouse except for Joe. He came in about an hour after we ate. Gene asked him.

"Where you go out there? We looked for a while and then gave up and came in and had supper. You better get up to the house and eat some of what's left.

"Well, boss I'll do that. One of those old ewes got stuck in that fence over north of here. I don't know how she got her head through that fence but it took a time to get her out."

Then I asked Dean to come with me to town for a drink. We hadn't told anyone about being shot at the night before. As we were riding into town Dean asked.

"Now Jim I've seen you in the Long Bar and I never seen you drink more than a glass of beer. So, why are we going to town?"

"I just hate to be shot at and I wouldn't want that person thinking we left the country. Now would you?"

"See what you mean and no I wouldn't. It's not in me to be run out of a place."

"That's what I wanted to hear. I'm going to cozy up to Lola see if she knows anything. Why don't you just hang around the bar and see if you can hear that voice we heard last night?"

We tied up at the hitching rail and made our way to the bar. As I thought Lola made her way to our side.

"What you boys doing in town on a week night?"

"Just wanted to let everyone know we still was in the country. Come on Lola and sit at the table. Doby, bring us two beers."

"Will do."

"Where's Ted, Lola?"

"He went somewhere, said he had important business out of town. Said he'd be back in a couple of days. Took some grub, must be camping out somewhere. Can't be a woman or he wouldn't need the grub. Now would he."

"Don't seem likely."

Dean stayed at the bar drinking his beer as Lola and me took a sit at a table.

"Lola, how did you ever start in this line of work?"

"Well that's a long story but I'll give you the short version. I was at home and sixteen and mother had married a man after pa had died. This man would come home after drinking in town and he would beat my mother. I would try to stop him and he would start beating on me. The last time I saw my mother was a year later when he came in all drunk and started in on my mother and I just couldn't get him to stop. She was all bloody and cut up. He let up and I went to her and she was dead. Well I was crying and he came after me but this time he was in a rage and tore off all my clothes and I knew what was going to happen so I grabbed a big skillet and hit him as hard as I could over the head. He dropped hard to the floor and I got some more clothes on and left and never looked back. I don't know if he was dead or not. I hate that I was too scared to stay and see my mother get proper buried. That was three years ago when Ted took me in and gave me this job. I'm sorry, I never told anybody that before not even Ted. I guess I let it all out cause there's something I like in you."

"Well, I'm right sorry about that trouble it seems that I like you to. You're a nice girl but you should get out of here and find something better."

"I don't know nothing else and any way Ted pays me extra to listen to the cowboys and let him know what they say. I shouldn't have told you that."

"That's alright I already could see that. Did you hear anything last night?

"Just you and Dean were leaving that's why I was surprised to see you in town."

"Who told you that?"

"Well Bart came in near closing time with a man and they talked to Ted and left. That's when he told me you two were gone and wouldn't be back."

"Who was the man with Bart?"

"I don't know. I never seen him but he was older and had on old clothes. Not dirty just old like from twenty or more years ago."

"Thanks Lola you're a great kid. Try to get out of here and do something with your life. You're so young and pretty to live this life and tell Ted we're not leaving.

"Come on Dean we better get back to the ranch."

I kissed Lola on the cheek and I got on Red and we were out of town. I couldn't sleep all night. The small bits of information that I had kept rolling around in my head and would not let me sleep. The next day I asked Dean if he knew an older man that dressed in old fashion clothes. It was in my mind the whole day working and by the end of the day I was dragging. After supper I fell in bed. The last thing I remember is Dean telling me he was going to town. When I woke up Pickin's and Dean was just sitting there staring at me.

"What is wrong with you two?"

Pickin's said, "We just never seen anyone sleep that long and sound. You better get up and get your horse. You missed breakfast you know."

"No!"

Dean said, "Yes you did."

I got up and I saddled Red and as we left the barn Sara and Bonnie ran out of the house and handed me a package.

"Didn't want you to go hungry before dinner."

"Thank you ma'am I'll try not to miss your delightful breakfast again."

Then we were away and I eat my breakfast in the saddle. That's when Gary came over.

"The one night you don't go to town and you sleep through breakfast and then my wife and daughter brings you eatin's in your saddle."

"And it's delicious boss. Can't wait till dinner."

"Do you mind if we get a little work done in between."

"No boss." I said as he turned and headed north and I could tell he was laughing under his breath then Dean, Pickin's and me headed west with our two dogs leading the way. I seemed to be all rested up and got more work done than I had in the two days before. By the end of the day Dean came over as we were riding in and struck up a conversation.

"You know last night when you were in la' la land and I went to town I saw something very interesting."

"What happened?"

"I was about to go in the Long Bar and as I looked over the bat-winged doors I saw Joe as big as life at the bar talking to Bart. I got back on my horse and waited around the edge of the building for half an hour. Joe came out with Bart and they headed west and I followed them way up in a canyon about twenty miles from town. I waited and waited and in about an hour they came out and went back toward town. After they headed back I went up the canyon and about ten minutes in you know what I found."

"No Dean, now come on tell me."

"I saw about fifty head of sheep and about seventy head of cattle and they were all fenced in a nice spot of grass and a small pond. Now I'm thinking what is Bart from Davis ranch and Joe from our ranch doing together with cattle and sheep all fenced in and at night. You know I seem to remember times when Bart was away from the ranch for two or three days at a time when I worked there and Tom would ask us if we seen him."

"The one night I don't go to town and all this happens."

"You think we should tell Gary and Tom?"

"No, not yet I'll let you know and we'll talk in town. You know there's more to this than you know about."

"Alright, but I hope you let me in on it."

We got back to the house and ate then Dean and me went to town. I had to see if June was in town. I needed to ask her some questions.

4

We were in no hurry so we were just pokin' along, the sun was just dropping behind one of the many mountains that were scattered throughout this part of Texas. It was a kind of flat land in between the mountains and sometimes a valley here or there but Dean was real quiet as we rode along.

"What you so quiet about Dean?"

"I was just thinking that I met you when you were trespassing on Tom's ranch and you know I liked you right away and you had no job and I was working for Tom and since then you got a job with Gary and I got fired by Bart and now I'm working with you."

"Now what in the world is wrong with that?"

"Nothing but now we find some cowhands stealing stock from both ranches. This all happened in two weeks. I'm just hoping that you aren't leading me into trouble that we can't get out of by getting shot or even hung for."

"Don't worry I never get in any trouble I can't get out of and I'm sure not going to get us hung by the law."

"Oh, I wasn't worried about the law as much as I was about the rustlers."

I started laughing and Red whinnied as we rode down the street of Alpine and stopped in front of the general store.

"What we doing in here?"

"I think someone might be in here that I need to talk to. You can go and get a drink at the Long Bar I'll meet you there later."

"Can't I come with you?"

"Not this time, she's kind of shy around people."

"Oh, she, now I find out the truth. You've been holding out on me."

"No, it's just a girl I met a few weeks ago before you stuck that rifle in my face out on Tom's ranch. She said she might see me in town sometime. She said to drop around the general store. You can meet her soon enough. You might like to get to know her better she might be your type more than mine."

"Alright, I'll see you later pard."

He walked his horse across the street to the Long Bar and went inside. That's when I tied Red to the hitching rail and went inside the general store. A bell rang as I opened the door and the man at the counter that was helping a mother and her young daughter looked my way.

"I'll be with you in a minute sir after I help these young ladies."

"Thank you, take your time I'm just looking around. I'll see if I find something I need."

"That's fine."

I looked around the store but did not see anyone else in sight. So I just kept looking at the ropes and the saddles with the bridles then the horse blankets. I heard the bell sound again and looked, as did the storeowner but there was no one in sight. He said to the mother.

"I guess it was the wind."

I was about to give up when something pulled on my shirt shelve and I looked around and down and there was June with a raincoat on and a hat pulled down over her eyes with her hair tucked up under her hat.

"June, you would be less suspicious if you dressed like that lady at the counter."

"Someone might recognize me. Meet me out back like before."

I told the storeowner I would be back after while and went out and around the corner and June was already there.

"What took you?"

"June, I don't know about you. You sure know how to get around without being seen."

"Never mind that, what you find out?"

"It's coming along. It doesn't happen overnight. I've found some rustling going on."

"You arrested them, they might be the ones that killed gramps."

"No, I need more evidence before I can do that and they might led us to the one that is behind all that happened. It just takes time June. I need to ask you some questions."

"Why ask me ask them?"

"If I ask the rustlers I would be giving myself away about what I'm doing here. Now did you see your grandpa dead?"

"What kind of question is that? Of course I did, I buried him in the tunnel of the mine."

"Okay, was there another man about your grandpa's age that was around when the town had people? Maybe a friend of his that dressed nice but older clothes."

"I don't know. That was a long time ago."

"I know but I need to know cause there is someone like that that maybe trying to scare us off."

"What you mean us? No one knows about me around here except Ted and he probably forgot me by this time. He's the one that believed gramps about the gold."

"I have someone working with me but he doesn't know I'm a Ranger or anything about the case. I'm going to have to tell him soon he's already asking why I'm doing all this."

"Are you sure about him? Can you trust him? Your and my life might depend on that trust."

"I know, that's why I'm waiting to tell him. This case is bigger than we thought and my Captain sure didn't know anything about it. I'll go slow and make sure of him. I better go I told him I'd meet him at the Long Bar."

"Wait Jim, when you said Long Bar it made me think about the saloon in Marfa when I was younger. Gramps told me of a man that he met in the saloon and sit and played cards with. If I know gramps he probably told too much when he drank. All I remember is gramps said the man had a rough voice. I don't know about his age or how he dressed but he said that he was a fine gambling man."

"Thanks, that might help. I'll see you next week or two. By the way have you seen anyone?"

No, but I've been in the mine all day and I sleep in my hideout at night. But I did see horse tracks in the street two days ago. But that could be any stranger."

"Just keep an eye out to see if any more of the same tracks show up."

I turned the corner and went across the street to the Long Bar. Dean was sitting at a table by the window that looked out to the general store. With him were Joe and Slim and Bob. I walked up to the boys.

"What are you boys doing in town this time of night?"

Slim said, "We get thirsty once in a while you know."

Then Joe said, "Dean said you have a girl."

Maybe this would be some bait and he might take it. I know June could hide out and not be seen anywhere.

"Could be, just a girl I met before coming here over near an old ghost town out about twenty miles from here. Said she was from a ranch around there."

"I know the place; I think it was named Marfa or something like that." Joe said.

Then Slim said, "Yelp, seemed I heard that some old coot over that way years ago was telling people that he knod where some yeller was."

I said. "You mean gold?"

"Sure thing, what else of importance is yeller except maybe a girl's hair." Bob said.

Everyone laughed and drank up their beer.

"I'm headin' for the ranch, today tuckered me out." I said.

Then Dean spoke. "Me to, it was a hard day. Y'all coming."

"No, think we'll hang around for another beer before headin' back."

"See y'all in the morning."

We rode out of town and Dean said.

"I saw that girl all dolled up in that raincoat and that hat pulled down over her face. What's she trying to hide?"

"Told you she was shy."

"Shy is one thing but that raincoat is another."

"Just leave it alone for now, alright."

"Sure thing, it's your business not mine unless it can get me killed."

"I'll tell you more when I can. Now let's get to the ranch and some good sleep."

As we were riding back to the ranch my mind kept wondering when and where the next shot might ring out to try to run us out of here. Someone didn't like new people here asking to many questions. The next morning Dean and me talked to Gary after breakfast when no one was around.

"You know Gary, Dean and me would like for you to take a little ride out west of here. It might be of interest to you."

"What is it?"

"You need to see it for yourself to believe it."

"All right let me tell the boys to go on without me."

"I think it would be a good idea if you just told them you have some important business to handle with Dean and me."

"Alright, but I hope it's worth my time."

As we were riding west and we soon were off Gary's ranch I could see a puzzled look on Gary's face.

"What could interest me over here this isn't on my ranch?"

"Just wait, if you notice it's not on Tom's ranch either." Dean put in.

We rode up the canyon where the sheep and cattle had been pinned up but when we reached the fenced area all the livestock were gone.

"Well, boys what's going on not much to see?"

"Gary, look here at this fence and look at the hoof prints. I know I'm new to this country but those are cattle and sheep prints around that pond. Just look."

Gary got off and was walking around the pond and pushed his hat back on his head and scratched his head and then looked up at us.

"Yelp, those are sure cattle and sheep tracks. Now boys what's going on around here?"

"Should I tell him about the other night Jim."

"Can't be helped now most of the evidence is gone."

"Well, Gary two night ago I went to town and I saw Joe talking to Bart in the Long Bar so I stopped and waited outside and followed them to this spot. They spent thirty minutes in here and went back to town. I told Jim the next day and we came here and there was about fifty sheep and seventy cattle. This happened after we got shot at the night I got my things from Tom's."

"Are you saying that Tom had you shot at and stole my sheep?"

I spoke up. "No, I don't think that Tom knows about any of this just like you didn't have any clue about this."

"Then what? Joe and Bart are getting rich off both of us. I can hardly believe that of Joe. Bart I can but not Joe."

"Money speaks loud. I think someone else is behind all this. I think, as yet I don't have much proof, that they want to get both your ranches by stealing you two blind and when you can't pay your mortgage they will buy it for a song. I'll have to investigate it more."

"Wait a minute you talk about proof and investigate more. That sounds like a lawman."

I reached in my pocket and pulled out my badge and held it to my chest. The look of amazement was all over both of their faces and I put it back in my pocket.

"A Ranger, I never had a clue."

"Me neither boss."

"How did you get wind of this?"

"I didn't until now I just stumbled onto this. I am here on another case but I think the two cases are both part of each other. Now I have been here a couple of weeks and I think I can trust both of you. I don't want this getting out yet we don't know if some more of your hands are involved or not but Gary if you would not tell anyone about this and you Dean will still help me I think I can solve your case and the other case givin' a month or so. For now we have to let Joe and Bart alone. Maybe we can catch them in the act of stealing or selling them."

"But they're stealing us blind and what is this other case."

"I can't say what the other case is right now but me and Dean can be out here at night and maybe catch Joe and Bart outright and no one will suspect anything about the other case for now. Will you two help me with this?"

Gary said, "If I can stop my sheep from being stolen I'm in."

"I am to but don't we need to let the sheriff know."

"Not yet, I don't know much about him and if he is involved in some way. We'll have to wait and see."

"We better get back to the ranch and get to work before someone get suspicious."

The way back was quiet but I was thinking all the way back. I knew that Dean and me weren't going to get much sleep the next month or two. I had an idea pop in my head.

"Gary, I have been kind of close with Pickin's. I think he's an honest man, I know he has that nasty habit but if he and Dean could rotate nights in that canyon it would help and don't tell him about me being a Ranger. I'll fill him in on the rest."

"When we get through for the day I'll tell him to get with you and Dean for some night patrol and not tell anyone else."

"That a do it for now."

We went back to work as usual and I knew the burden was on me now to prove the murder case. I knew we would catch the stock thief's now with the help. We also had to keep an eye in town and on the trail to Marfa to see who was going over that way trying to locate the gold mine. This last part would fall on me for now. There were still a lot of unknowns but I have seen much more difficult cases before. Now that Gary was with me I could be gone for a day or two on so-called ranch business without much suspicion. Now to get Pickin's on our side. That night when we were sitting on our bunks I ask Pickin's if Gary said anything to him.

"Sure did, he said, I was to talk to you about helping you and Dean at night."

"We don't want this to get around and we think we can trust you not to tell anyone else."

"You know you can if it's to help Gary and his family."

"It is, we think someone here and at Tom's ranch is stealing both ranches stock and Dean and me found where they are holding the stock but they were gone. So we need to catch them there with the stock so Dean is out there tonight and you'll be there tomorrow night and don't tell anyone what we're doing."

"You can count on me."

So I took off to town and Dean went to the canyon and I was going to try to make the pieces of the puzzle come together. As I rode down the street I could see the lights in the Long Bar but not much more was going on after dark although there was a light in the sheriff's office. I knew I had to find out something about John Brady and if he in some way might be involved so I turned Red to the sheriff's office and started inside. As I walked to the door I could hear voices so I stopped to listen awhile. Two voices that I didn't recognize but I was sure one was John Brady and the other sounded familiar although I couldn't place it.

"I heard that since Dean left Tom's ranch that stock had seem to be missing."

"Where you hear that? I've had no reports of the sort. I don't know how you hear things cause you only been here a week or so."

"Well you know one hears things around the poker table if you keep your ears open and I heard things on the trail when I came from El Paso."

"I don't know how ain't much out that way 'cept desert and the like."

"Well there is that small town a ways from here Marfa. I seemed to have talked to two boys over there from over this way that had some real information. You know in my business I file it away for future use."

"So you say. Who and why would someone from here be in that old ghost town? Any way I wouldn't rouse Dean on no hear say from any old saddle bum. He's always been an upstanding young man. I like him."

"I don't have a clue why they were over there and I didn't ask their names. All right but don't say I didn't warn you. Now good night."

I stepped back around the corner and waited until he left. He stopped on the boardwalk and eyed my horse and looked around while he lit his cigar and threw the match in the street near my horse. Red just stood there and did not make a move and the man moved on and went to the Long Bar. I watched as he turned and looked my way for a minute then turned and went to the bar. This is when I took a step to the door and went in to talk to John Brady.

"Hello Sheriff Brady, I just dropped in to talk to you a few minutes."

He looked up from his paper work and from this close up I thought my eyes were deceiving me. When I had seen him in the Long Bar it had been from a distance of more than seventy feet and I had only seen him for a few seconds. But I had thought for only a split second that I knew him but I didn't recognized the name. But from this close up there was no doubt about who I was looking at. It was one of the famous old Texas Ranger Tim Dolan. I reached out my hand and he shook it.

"Well I'll be what are you doing here Tim with that new handle."

"First I thought it was customary to come by the laws office when a Ranger comes into a new town."

"Well, if I had known it was you I would have but you know in some towns the law can be in deep with the one's being investigated. Now how about that name."

"Don't give me away but I just thought with my reputation as a Ranger there would be to many eyes watching me all the time. About the same reason you had not come to me when you came to town two weeks ago."

"I see what you mean."

"I telegraphed John in Austin and he didn't know much but that you were here."

"He got a strange letter from near here about a murder. That's all we knew till I got here. I know more now but I was worried if I sent a telegram it might get into the wrong hands."

"Why you come in to see me now?"

"Because I have run into more than murder but I think they are connected somehow. Not for sure yet."

"So what's goin' on?"

"I've found some sheep and cattle rustling going on and we found where they are holding them till they sell them."

"Who are we?"

"Dean and Gary. Dean found where the stolen stock was and I saw them for myself but when we took Gary over there the stock was gone. I came in to tell John, now I know it's you, we are setting up a trap when they bring more stolen stock in that place. So in the next few days you might be receiving some prisoners."

"Do you think Tom is mixed up in this?"

"I'm pretty sure he's not cause one of Gray's men and one of Tom's men have been seen with the stolen stock. The men and the stock were all together and right now I don't think Tom would have anything to do with sheep."

"That sure is the truth. He has tried to get me to arrest Gary but I told him the same thing that Gary wouldn't have anything to do with cattle. Do you think that those men are the only ones involved?"

"No I don't. I think someone is pitting the two ranchers against each other. Right now I don't know who that is but I'm thinking that the arrest of his two men will make him show his hand."

"You mention a murder?"

"Yes, that's another case but I think they are linked together somehow. You know how that goes I just have a feeling about it. I better get back to the ranch; good to know you're here. That's one less worry I have. Oh, before I forget who was that man in here before me?"

"He's just an old gambler that came to town about a week ago. He seems to try to butt into everyone business. His name is Chance Larson if you can believe that. Who was murdered?"

"You know how that goes. I have to keep track of everyone. I'll fill you in later when I know more. You know the less people that know the less I have to keep track of. So long Tim I mean John. Just keep this all under your hat."

"Sure thing if you keep my little secret."

We both laughed and I shook his hand and walked out the door. I hopped on Red and rounded the corner and sat there a while and watched. John left his office and walked down the street checking the doors of the businesses and then after two blocks he opened the gate of a house and went to the door and took off his hat and went inside without knocking. That must be his house. So I turned Red and went down the street toward the ranch. When I turned in Dean was fast asleep and so was I when my head hit that nice soft pillow.

When I woke Pickin's was talking to Gary. I looked over at Dean.

"What's that all about?"

"Pickin's want's Gary to explain to Gene why he was out all night and needs to get some sleep. Seems Gene didn't believe him."

"Well here comes Gene. Does he look mad?"

"Na, just a little upset."

"Good. I wouldn't want to get on his wrong side."

"Dean, Jim what's going on, the boss said I should talk to you two?"

"Just we saw some suspicious tracks the other night, there were sheep and cattle tracks together so I told the boss and he put Dean and Pickin's rotating every other night until we find out what's going on."

"You should have let me know?"

"I'm sorry, being new we just went to the boss. I sure thought he would tell you."

"I see your point. Let's get to breakfast and then out on the range. Maybe you can show me those tracks later."

"Sure thing." Dean said.

I told Dean. "Don't tell him too much and I'm going to tell Gary that I'm going to be gone a few days. I'm sure he'll make some kind of excuse with Gene until we can let him in on all the goings on's."

After breakfast I talked to Gary and then went to town. I still had no lead to who had killed Guy Grayson and if it was the same person that was going to Marfa looking for June and the gold mine. I was coming around a bend between two large boulders when I heard the sound of some horses so I rode Red up and around the boulder where I could see who it might be. There were three of them. One was Chance that I had seen the night before and one of the other two men was Shorty that rode for Tom's ranch. The third I didn't recognize but he had the looks of a cowhand. They rode pass where I was and it looked to me that they had no concern that someone might be following them as I now was for what would two cowhands be doing with an old gambler out on the trail heading west out of town. This might be a long stretch of my imagination but I had nothing else to go on. I had my spyglass with me so I hung back as they rode out from among the boulders and out on the open prairie. This was the road to Marfa. The prairie grass was aplenty out here and the cactus was along the trail but not much else to hide behind. They still were not checking their back trail but I still tried to keep the dust down but it was hard in this arid place. The road, if it could be called that, to Marfa was coming up but as I watched them they turned the opposite way toward the mountains. I didn't know where June's mine was but I knew that she would be there now.

I hurried along as the men disappeared into a canyon. It came to me to try to reach the rim so I headed Red up the side of the canyon but it became too steep and I had to leave Red on a level spot and hook it on foot. It was all of another hundred feet and mostly loose slate. For every two steps I would slide back one. With rifle in hand I made it to the rim. There I could make out the three rides with my spyglass. It looked like they were looking for an opening and tracks. They would get off their horses and walk looking at the ground then would pull back any loose vegetation on the canyon wall. I had my rifle ready if they found her. I was sure I could hit all three from here if I thought they were going to harm June. After about an hour with no luck finding anything they looked like they got into a heated argument. They were now leaving the canyon with no luck finding what they were looking for so I made my way down to where Red was and mounted and was on their trail back to Alpine. I made a detour down the road to Marfa and came into the street of the town as the sun was headed down to the horizon. There was no sign of June of course but I knew she would find me. I was by the horse trough letting Red get a well-deserved drink and I was pouring water over my head and Red looked up and whinnied as June came out of the hotel.

"What you doing here Jim? Kind of a hot day to be out this far."

"Now June, I was just doing my job. Followed three fellows all the way from Alpine. One was that old man that I was asking you about his name is Chance Larson. He's a gambler and I don't know what else but it looked like they were searching for you or your mine. One of the others was Shorty, he works at the Davis ranch. The third man I didn't know."

"That would be Bud Timas. I'd seen them coming. It's not the first time I've seen them. They keep looking but they are a long ways from where the mine is. It's pretty well hidden. I wouldn't know if that was the same man that my grandpa played poker with but if he has a real rough voice it could be, he looks to be old enough. Never been close enough to hear him."

"Well, I don't know but Dean and me were shot at the other night and that someone with a usual voice told us to leave and not come back. We thought it to be Bart but it wasn't his voice."

"Maybe they're working together."

"That well may be, this case has so many angles. You mind if I spend the night it's a far piece back."

"Sure Jim, your room is always ready at the top of the stairs in the hotel. I'll make you some supper and breakfast in the morning. I have to keep in practice after this is over I might find a young man that will help me revive this old town."

"Could be."

After I took care of Red while June was fixing supper we sat down and ate. She talked about her childhood with her grandpa after her mother and father had died in this town. I told her about some of my assignments after becoming a Texas Ranger and how I liked helping good people with difficult situations. I said goodnight and headed up to my room in the hotel but I still didn't know where she lived. I guess it takes her a long time to really trust someone but I was sure that she would be safe.

The next morning Red was saddled and breakfast was on the table in the hotel diner. After we ate and I mounted Red I told June,

"Now, you be careful I hope we can get this wrapped up in a month or so."

With that I rode out of town and was down the trail to Alpine. I got back early in the afternoon so I went out to the range and found Dean and Pickin's working as if nothing was happening other than work. The dogs were doing their job of rounding up the sheep making them go where the men wanted them to. Dean rode over to me as the afternoon wore on.

"Where you spend last night your bunk sure looked awful empty."

"I just went out to see that gal that you saw me with in town."

"The one in the raincoat the shy one. She must be becoming a little less shy around you."

"Come on Dean its business with her. I don't really know where she lives. I just show up and she finds me."

"Well, I'll be, I wish I had a gal that would come running to find me when I wanted her to."

Pickin's had ridden up about that time and they were both having a good laugh at my expense. I knew it was all in fun but I did turn colors for a while.

"How did it go last night out at the canyon?" Pickin's started to speak up as he was withdrawing his finger from his nose.

"Nothing was goin' on over there. I nearly fell asleep in the saddle. You sure there is something goin' on. I sure do miss my bunk every other night."

"Don't worry, I'm sure something will happen in the next few nights and then you can be in your bunk every night. Any way it's Dean's turn tonight while I'm in town. I will join you later."

We rode in with the dogs in the lead after getting the sheep to another pasture just in time to meet up with Gary and the other men. Gary came over.

"Jim, we saw some tracks that weren't any of our boys and there were two sets of dog tracks that weren't our dogs. That puzzles me cause they have to be a special train dog to herd sheep. I just wonder where they would keep them. I'm sure Tom wouldn't have such dogs on his place."

"You know Gary, that I don't think that Tom knows anything about this just like you didn't know. You been keeping an eye on Joe."

"Yelp, he works all day. He goes off once in a while but he's been back within thirty minutes or so. But last night when the lights were out in the house I stayed up and saw him leave out the back way. Could be to town I thought but he was back in an hour. That's not enough time to get to town and back and have a few drinks."

"He may be meeting someone on the trail to make plans. Maybe when he's working and not in your sight he's moving some sheep over to some grass where he knows they'll stay so they can get them faster when they want them."

"You know he did have Toby with him today. Jim, I just thought there is an old line shack on the northeast side of the ranch that they might be keeping some dogs. We don't use it much except in the winter months."

"I'll check it out tonight before I go to town. If I see anything I'll leave them alone. We want to catch them in the act."

"I'll tell Dean and Pickin's to come get you and the boys if anything breaks. They will need help we wouldn't want them to get away."

We reached the house by the time Sara was out front calling us for supper.

"Where you been Jim? I heard a rumor that you have a gal."

I looked over at Dean and Pickin's and they were laughing.

"Just a friend, Sara."

"That's how it starts. Now isn't that right?"

"Now Sara, leave Jim alone."

"Oh, pa just funnin' with him."

We sat down and ate and Bonnie's cooking was great as usual. Bonnie spoke up.

"That gal must fix a find supper and breakfast to keep you away from my cooking'."

Everyone was laughing then Gary said.

"Not you to Bonnie leave Jim alone."

"Ma'am she is a right good cook but not like yours. I assure you of that."

Now Jim and Bonnie were also laughing.

"Well Jim, that's a sure compliment. Thank you."

I got out of the house without turning to many colors. Dean and me left and I left Dean at the cutoff to the canyon and went on to town. As I rode up the street to the Long Bar I saw John in front of his office and he tipped his hat to me as I rode by. When I went inside all the suspects were there. Bart, Ted and Chance then over in the corner were Shorty and the other man that was searching the canyon. I walked up to the bar and ordered a beer when Ted came up with Chance.

"Jim, I don't think you know Chance."

"No, not from this distant and not in the light."

"Well, sir what is that to mean?"

Sure enough there was that deep, rough voice that I was expecting.

"Anything you want it to mean. You can see that I'm still in the country and I'm not leaving anytime soon."

"Now, now gentlemen lets have no trouble in here."

"Ted, I wouldn't think of starting any trouble and doing any damage to this beautiful long bar or that mirror behind it."

"I thank you for that. Now you two have a drink on me."

Chance said. "Any way could I get you to play a game of poker."

"Might just could."

"Ted, join us and you two over there come on."

Everyone came over and we took a seat at a table. I took my beer with me. I wasn't going to have another one.

Ted said, "Jim this is Shorty he works for Bart at Toms ranch and this here is Fred from over Denver way. He came in with Chance about a week ago."

Now from up close I recognized him from a wanted poster I had seen at the Ranger office in Austin he was Fred Ward and he was wanted for bank robbery and murder. But this wasn't the time or place for an arrest. I was sure that would come later. Ted started to deal and we all had our money out in front of us. We were playing five-card stud and I had one ace and two fours, a jack and a ten. Chance opened for a dollar and everyone tossed his dollar in the pot and called. I took two cards and was rewarded with another ace and another four. I noticed that Ted had dealt me two cards from the bottom of the deck. I pretended not to notice. Ted bet five dollars and everyone called but me I raised him ten dollars. I was sure I was dealt this hand so I could win to get my confident up so later they could steal me blind. Ted and Chance stayed in and called me. I showed my hand with a big smile. I won the pot. I wanted them to think I was a fool.

I won two more hands that were dealt in the same manner as before. Then Shorty and Fred left the game and we three kept playing. As the game continued Chance won two hands then Ted won one. Then I noticed that Bart and Shorty had slipped out of the saloon. I was ahead by a couple of hundred dollars and I knew it was going to be hard to get away but I had a feeling that I needed to, so the next two deals I just through my hands in when I knew I would win. I told Ted I had to leave and him and Chance tried to keep me there and as I got up to leave I turned toward the door and Fred tried to block my way.

"Where you think you're going?"

"I have to go to work early I need to get some sleep. I'll give y'all another go around at me another night."

Fred said, "I don't think so, sit down."

I turned back toward Ted and Fred stepped in closer to my back and I heard his gun clear leather so I turned quick and grabbed Fred's wrist and twisted the gun from his hand into mine and hit him over the head with his own gun barrel and he fell to the floor like a ton of lead. Then I was back facing Chance and Ted with the gun pointing right at their faces.

5

There was a surprise look that came over Chance's face as I backed out of the Long Bar. Red was ready and I was in the saddle and out of town in a matter of minutes. I knew where to go and the line shack was on the north end of Gary's ranch so I rode in slow and there was a light coming from the window so I dismounted and went down a gully that went to the back of the cabin as I looked in I could hear two men in front of the cabin saying to get the dogs out and head to the Thomas ranch. As I left I peered into the window and there were two dogs so I made it back to Red and we hi-tailed it toward the canyon. The way Red was galloping along, before I knew the cut to the canyon was coming up. It was dark but Red knew where and what he was doing. As I started to take a left into the canyon there was someone coming toward me that I could not tell who it was until they got right up to me.

It was Dean so Red slowed up and Dean said that they just came into the canyon but only with fifty or so cattle and he was going to get Gary.

"You go on, I'm going to Tom's and get more help. I just left the line shack and they were leaving to get the sheep with the dogs and they weren't our dogs but one of the men was Joe."

"You think Tom will come."

"You get Gary and the boys I'll take care of Tom."

Dean headed towards our ranch and I headed Red toward Tom's ranch. I knew Tom had to see for himself what was going on or he would never believe it. Red was going at top speed like he knew the way and what was up ahead. I didn't slow him for I had every confidence in my horse. As I passed the gate of the ranch I pulled my rifle out of the scabbard and fired just two shots. By the time I reached the house Tom was on the front porch with rifle in hand and the bunkhouse was all lit up. I jumped off Red and ran up to the porch. Tom had his rifle pointing right at my face.

"What you mean coming in here like that? I could have shot you."

"Tom, we have the rustlers in a box canyon east of here. Dean has gone to get Gary. You might want to come and see who's been steeling your cattle and Gary's sheep. There's not much time we'll talk later."

"Boys get the horses we're going to a hanging party."

In five minutes everyone was mounted then someone said.

"Boss what if it's a trick that those sheep herders set up."

I said. "Tom we don't have time for this, let's go now."

I let Red have his head and he took off out of the Davis ranch. As we rode along at top speed I yelled over the sound of the horses hoofs and the powerful wind in our face.

"Gray should be getting there about the same time we do. This is one time you two better work together and there won't be any hanging till there's a trial. They will get their just do. John will see to that."

I slowed down and yelled.

"The way into the canyon is just up ahead. I don't hear any shooting so Gary and his men aren't here yet but listen, hear the cattle bawling in there."

"I hear some sheep loud and clear."

"Look here comes Dean and the men."

I stopped Dean and Gary and told them.

"As we go in some of you go to the right and some to the left. Dean, you and me and Tom and Gary will go down the middle."

Tom says, "Hello Gary." Then comes.

"Hello Tom, we have to get all of them. Jim and Dean knows one of our men, Joe is involved and one of yours, he said Bart. We don't know who else so look over your men so we won't be shooting our good men."

"I can't believe Bart."

"Tom, that's why he fired me cause I thought something was going on. Then that night he fired me I think it was him that shot at me and Jim on the trail." Dean told Tom.

"Let's go on in boys. Now we're in this together? We don't know how many are in there."

We took off down the mouth of the canyon and we could hear the sounds of dogs barking and voices of men along with the bawling of the sheep and the deep low moo's of the cattle. We four went right down the middle of the canyon and Gary's men went to the left and Tom's went to the right. The cattle and sheep with the dogs barking out orders to the sheep were so loud that the men didn't detect us till we were on them then all hell broke loose. They let loose with enough firepower for ten men and then we started firing back, trying not to hit any stock or our own men. There looked to be about six men then I spotted Joe.

"Gary, there's Joe over there."

"Don't worry I'll get him."

Tom yelled, "Over there, I see Bart. I'll get him."

"I'll help you." I said.

We rode though the cattle and sheep right at Bart and he saw us and took off to the other side of the canyon.

I yelled, "Tom, there must be another way out over there."

"I'll try to head him off you go right for him."

I looked back and the others along with Joe had been rounded up with one or two on the ground and I was out another cut after Bart with Tom right behind me. I was not twenty feet behind Bart so I got my lasso and shook out a loop and let it fly when I got within ten feet of him. Red knew to stop and pull back and that made Bart fly backwards off his horse. He was up on his feet trying to get the rope off. I got off Red just when he got the rope off and I saw Tom come up. He took a swing at me that I ducked and the swing took him back in the dirt.

Tom yelled. "Give up Bart."

"What and hang, no thanks."

As Bart started to get up I saw him drawing his gun and I pulled mine and shot him right in the gut above his belt buckle. He fell in the dirt and rolled over dead. Tom walked over and looked down.

"I saw him go for his gun. I knew he was mean but I never thought he was this bad."

We put Bart across his horse and went back into the canyon. The two men I saw on the ground had been put across their horses and the other two were hog-tied and on their horses ready for the ride to the sheriff's office. Tom said,

"Toby, get Sam and Todd and take the cattle back to the ranch. The rest of you can help then hit your bunk. Looks like the cattle rustling is over."

"Sure thing boss, you want us to take the dead and bury them."

"No, boys we'll leave that to John." Then Gary said.

"Pickin's, you, Bob and Slim get the sheep back to the ranch and see what you can do for those poor sheep dogs. They look starved and need water. We're going to town."

"Sure, Gary we'll take care of everything."

"Come on Jim, you and Dean come with Tom and me. Jim you know how to handle this."

I told the two ranchers. "Look you two at the cattle and sheep, they seem to get along fine together. It's just the ranchers that can't get along. Did you know Tom, I've been studying about the sheep since I went to work for Gary, the sheep eat the grass lower to the ground than cattle but that makes it grow back faster and taller."

We headed to town with three dead men and two for the courts. We rode along nice and easy. The horses needed the rest and it was never pleasant killing men.

"Joe, what made you do this?" Gary said. "Was it the money?"

"I don't know boss. At first I said no and was going to tell you then I started thinking about having my own ranch. He was going to give me twenty per cent but he never did. So I guess I was the fool. I'm really sorry boss."

"I am to Joe but you went too far."

I said. "Do you Joe or you Shorty know who else is in this. I know Bart wasn't smart enough to plan all this. He wasn't ever gone long enough to sell the stock."

Joe said. "I sure don't know."

Shorty kept his mouth shut.

Tom said. "Shorty, you think the one you're trying to protect is going to get you out of this mess. If you tell us I'll try, mad as I am, to kept you from hanging just time in prison."

Shorty said. "I don't know anything and I'll get out some way. They're not going to hang me."

We stopped in front of the sheriff's office about midnight and I said.

"I'll be right back. I'll get John."

I walked down the street with Dean and we went up to John's house and knocked on the door.

"He's going to be real happy to see us this time of night." I kind of laughed and then the door opened and a red eyed man with his hair all messed up stood in front of us.

"Go back to sleep dear it's just a couple of old cowhands. I'll see what they want. Y'all better have a good reason wakin' us up this time of night."

"We do John, better get you shirt, boots and hat, it might take a while down at your office."

"Just a minute, I should have known with you in town I wouldn't get no rest."

John came out and we walked down the street and as we got closer John said.

"Three dead and two alive."

"That about sums it up."

"Hello Tom, Gary looks like y'all been busy tonight."

"Busier than we would like."

He looked at each of the dead men and said.

"Dean, would you take those three to the undertaker and wake him up and then take the horses to the livery. Put them in a stall and take off their gear and feed and water them. They look 'bout done in."

"Sure thing John."

"Joe, what got into you and Shorty? I knew you hung around Bart too much, bring them in the office and we'll get them a room."

"Well, I seemed to recall you had a few drinks with Bart."

"That's my job, trying to get the low-down on things that might happen around here."

Gary spoke up. "John, I'll let Jim tell you the whole story. Him and Dean found out about all this."

As I was telling John the whole story I could see Tom and Gary outside talking and shaking their heads once in a while. Then I saw them shake hands.

"You know John this I just stumbled on I am still on a murder case. So I'll be here awhile. Look at those two outside shaking hands."

"I never thought I'd see that. Now next time make your arrest in the daylight."

"That's a deal. I'll just keep them tied up until the sun is up."

We were both laughing when Tom and Gary came in. Then Dean came up the street into the office.

"Jed was real happy with me but we got it taken care of. He said he would sell their horses and belongings to pay for their burial."

"That's fine, I figured he would."

"Now y'all get out of here so I can go get some sleep. I'll take care of those two in the morning."

Tom said. "One more thing and we'll be out of your hair. Gary and me decided to try to live next to each other like good neighbor."

"That's great now get out of my hair."

As the four of us rode out of town two hours later Tom stopped and turned in his saddle.

"Gary, why did you say to Jim back there that you would let him explain everything."

"I'll leave it to him to tell you if he can now."

I pulled my badge out of my pocket and pinned it on my shirt.

'Well I'll be, never would have guess. Why didn't you tell me?"

"I only told Gary and Dean three days ago and with Bart working for you I just wasn't sure about you. This is just between us four so don't tell anyone cause as a told John I'm still on a murder case and I think someone in this town is responsible. That's all I can say right now. I just stumbled onto this by accident but I'm sure glad I did. Now you two may become friends."

"I sure hope so, I'll tell all my boys to leave you and your men alone. But I still don't like sheep."

We were all laughing as we parted ways with Tom.

Next morning I woke up and there was Pickin's and Dean looking at me.

"That was sure some goings on last night." Pickin's said as he left for the outhouse.

Now Dean had a more down to earth comment.

"What are we going to do now?"

"Dean, that's been on my mind all night. I think we'll go out with the boys and do a little work. I do some of my best thinking when I'm working."

"Work when you have a murder case to solve."

"So you like that work, do you?"

"Sure!"

"Well, you know it takes time and a lot of thinking. I have to try to think like a killer. What he was thinking when he did the crime? And what he hoped to gain? Then how he thought he could get away with it. But right now we better get to breakfast or we might miss out."

At breakfast Sara was looking at Dean and me like we were some strange objects that fell to earth from the heavens.

"Dean, you and Jim were so brave last night."

"Sara, your father and the rest of the men were there also."

"I know but you two solved the trouble just like a real Texas Ranger."

"We just happen to be at the right place at the right time. Any ways it was Dean that found where they were keeping the stock. I was fast asleep that night."

"I know Dean you're so wonderful."

"Alright girl, that will be enough."

"Oh pa. I was just saying."

"Well boys we better get out to work."

Pickin's said. "Boss how about those two dogs from last night."

"Bring them, we'll see what they can do and if we can use them."

As we were walking to the barn Gary spoke to me. "I thought you would now be all into that other case."

"I need some time to think about that and I can think and work at the same time and now that Joe is in jail you need the help."

"That's for sure, I'll need to hire some more help with sheering coming up in a few weeks."

"I'd like to see that. I think I'll be around that long. But you understand that there will be times when I'll have to be away."

"Sure, like before."

We were out on the range and we took one of the new dogs and Gary took the other.

"Would you look at that, that new dog knows just how to work those sheep. Look at him chasing that rabbit and still handles the sheep.

I know we'll call him Gamer."

We watched as the dogs worked the sheep over to the new pasture with high grass. The dogs knew just where to take them when we opened the gate. I thought that this would be a good way to spend my old age but right now I had other things to do and tonight I was going to town and Dean was coming with me. We met up with Gary at noon and headed for the house.

Pickin's said, "Boss that new dog was workin' real good. I named him Gamer cause he did all that there chasing sheep and still he went after every rabbit he saw."

"Then that female we have we should name Sleeper. Every time the sheep settled down she would lay down in the shade and go to sleep."

"Did you notice boss; I think she's going to have pups. We might not want to work her so hard." Slim said.

Gray looked closer when we got to the house.

"You know Slim I think you might just be right. I'll tell Sara and she can keep her around the house till the pups come. Maybe now that the thieving has stopped our herd will increase faster so we might need some more dogs by the time those pups get big enough to train."

With the late night we were all done in by the time the day was over but I changed my shirt and looked over at Dean.

"You coming Dean,"

"Sure, I'm all tuckered out but I'll come."

"Keep this to yourself but I'm making you my assistant."

His eyes brightened up and he was up and ready for action.

"What do I do?"

"Let's go and I'll tell you."

On the road to town I told him.

"You just follow my lead and watch everyone around us and don't accuse anyone of anything. Just act like we'll regular sheep herders and watch that gal Lola. Don't tell her anything. We'll learn more if they don't know I'm a Ranger."

We stopped in front of John's office and went inside.

"Not you again. I hope you don't have any more criminals for me."

"No, just wondering if those two said any more."

"Joe now he talks all the time but nothing important and Shorty he just won't say anything except when Lola came in with their breakfast and dinner. That's funny how she knew they were here to bring breakfast? Never knew them to be close. But Shorty talked to her but I don't know what was said. At least my wife won't have to cook for them."

"Thanks we'll see you around."

"Remember no more midnight gatherings."

"Come on Dean let's see what's happening at the Long Bar."

We tied our horses at the hitch rail in front of the saloon and went inside. The sun was just going down and the inside was a lot cooler. We went to the bar and got some drinks and headed for a table. That's when Ted came out of the back room with Lola and he walked up to us looking kind of nervous.

"Can I sit down Jim?"

"Sure, draw up a chair."

"I just wanted to tell you; I don't know what got into Fred last night but I hope you don't think that I was trying to keep you here away from that canyon."

"Why would I think that?"

"I'm glad. I better get back to work."

"I thought you was the boss and owned all this."

"Well, I only own thirty percent Lola owns the rest."

He left and I looked at Dean.

"I'll be and I was feeling sorry for her. Keep that to ourselves."

"I never knew. Here she comes."

Lola walked up and pulled out a chair and sat down.

"Some going on last night. Saw you two bring in that bunch last night. We were just closing up."

"I hear you took them breakfast."

"Yep, I thought John's wife might be too busy. So I took them their meals. I knew both of them. I just felt sorry for them."

"That's good of you. Where's Chance and Fred?"

"Haven't seen them. You going to buy me a drink or I'll have to leave."

"Over here bring the lady a drink."

"Thought about leaving here and starting a new life?"

"I don't know I like it here and I like sleeping late whenever I can."

"I guess it could be rewarding around here with Ted giving you extra for information."

"It pays pretty well to keep my ears open. Dean that's our little secret."

"I thought so. I don't have much to tell anyone about anyways. Those sheep keep us pretty busy."

"So Jim, how you find out about what was going on out there?"

"Just a lucky guess and being at the right place at the right time. Sometime things just fall into place. No planning at all. Lola who's that man at the bar in the suit and derby hat cause I noticed that he hasn't paid for any drinks. He seems to drink a lot."

"That's the banker Sid Whasworth. He's the one that loaned Ted the money for this place and the interest is that he gets free drinks."

"That's lucky for him cause he seems to drink a lot."

"I better get over there before he drinks us dry and send him home to his wife."

Lola went over and talked to Sid and he stumbled out of the bar and I saw out the window him fall in the street on his face.

"You know Jim I never seen him drink that much before."

"We may have to watch him. His drinking all of a sudden may have to do with last night. Let's head back to the ranch."

As we rode along I told Dean.

"I've been thinking, you go get some sleep. I'm going out west of here. Tell Gary I'll be on business a couple of days."

"You sure you don't need me."

"Not this time. I think Gary needs your help more than I do right now. Later when I get closer to the answer then we'll be working together."

Dean took the cut off to the ranch and I headed for the canyons near Marfa. I was a little worried about June. I took the trail toward the west. It was a starry night and the trail was easy to follow. About midnight I found a likely place and set up a small dry camp. I unsaddled Red and tied him close by. I knew he would warn me if someone came around and I was off the trail a few hundred yards. After the goings on last night I had no trouble falling asleep. Red moving around woke me about five hours later. It was hard to see till my eyes adjusted to the dark. Then I saw two figures going west pass me. When they were a ways off I got Red saddled and headed behind them. They weren't traveling very fast in the dark but within a couple of hours it was starting to get light so I dropped back a ways from them. By the time it was full daylight and I could see it was Chance and Fred and they were winding their way through the buildings in Marfa not right down Main Street and I was a might closer. I didn't know where June was but I hoped she was out of sight. They dismounted and drew their guns looking inside each building to no avail but that didn't stop them. They finally brought their horses in and gave them hay and water and unsaddled them, they were here to stay awhile. They went and sat in front of the saloon and I was camped out in my old hotel room and Red was tied out behind some boulders with a small pond that June kept the weeds and grass out of. I was just going to have to wait them out and see what was going to happen. I never saw June all day. I sure was glad that I brought my canteen with me. It was so hot I felt like my skin was crawling. I knew June was around somewhere for the town was just as clean as it was when I first had seen it. I wondered how she found enough time to work in the mine and keep this town so clean. Then I saw a movement right about sundown and Fred went to see what it was down the street beside the livery. Then I heard a yell and Chance with gun in hand went toward where Fred was. Then they came from the back of the building and Fred was covered from head to toe with mud. He was shaking his hat out and took out his gun and it was full of mud. He handed it to Chance and jumped in the horse trough. When he got out I heard him yell at Chance.

"Let's get out of this ghost town. Whatever hit me wasn't alive."

"That doesn't make any sense. Someone has to be here look how clean everything is we'll leave in the morning."

"No sir I'm leaving right now."

Fred saddled his horse and left town with Chance right behind him. I was trying to keep from laughing till they were out of town when the door to my room opened and there was June with herself all wet and muddy. Then I busted out laughing and so did June.

"I got all wet when I pushed him in that mud puddle I made during the day."

We just kept laughing. Then I heard a noise and she heard it to. It was already dark inside and out and I hoped we could not be heard from where they were coming back down the street. I whispered.

"June, stay here I'm going to see what they're up to."

I closed the door behind me and creeped down the stairs and out the back door. The ally was dark and the moon had not come out. I worked my way to the corner of the hotel and around to the stable. There was nothing in there so I headed to where I had Red tied. Nothing yet maybe it was our imaginations but I didn't think so. As I came to the pond where I tied Red all of a sudden I realized that there was another horse there beside Red and I recognized the horse. It was Dean's and so I untied them both and walked them to the livery. There I unsaddled them both and gave them both a measure of oats and walked out in the street toward the hotel. I still was on the lookout cause I didn't want to get shot by Dean on accident. I started to call when I heard something down in back of the general store. When I got near I heard all this yelling and raving and then I was grabbed by the arm and pulled into the ally.

"I got whoever it is. They're in my mud hole in back of the store."

"Come on June, I think I know this one he's a friend."

We walked to the back of the store and there in the moon light I saw someone all covered in mud trying to get out of the mud hole. I went up to the mud hole and held out my hand.

"Take my hand Dean."

He looked up and I was trying not to laugh but he looked so funny that I busted out laughing. He grabbed my hand and I pulled and pulled and finally he came out grabbing his hat on the way and he just stood there looking at me with an angry look on his muddy face. Then he saw June without her raincoat on.

"Hello, ma'am, I'm Dean a friend or so-called friend of that one that is standing there laughing at me."

"You do look funny." She said trying not to laugh.

"What you doing here? I left you to go to work tomorrow. What will Gary think?"

As we guided him to the water trough to get the mud off he said.

"I thought you might run into trouble so I told Gary that you needed my help over here for a few days."

He took his gun out and got in the water and all the mud started coming off. I saw the look in June's eyes as the mud came off. She was just staring at Dean.

I said, "June you alright? There was no answer. "June" I said again and she snapped out of it.

"Yes Jim, what is it?

"This is Dean. Dean this is June."

As he got out he shook her hand.

"Good to meet you. I think I saw you in Alpine but I couldn't see your face. You were in a raincoat. Now I can see how pretty you are."

"Oh yes, that was me. But I'm not pretty, look at me dressed in my grandpa's old clothes. Here, come over to the hotel and I'll get you a towel and I'll find some of my grandpa's clothes for you to wear until yours dry."

Dean picked up his gun and we went to the hotel. She put him in the room next to mine and left to get some dry clothes.

"Dean, you could have gotten yourself killed. Chance and his gunfighter just left town."

"Yes, I saw them and they looked like there was a herd of cattle chasing them. I don't think anyone could have stopped them short of shooting them out of the saddle."

"This here is a ghost town and you fell into the same mud hole that June pushed him in. He didn't see her so he must had thought it was a ghost for they lit out of here."

June came back with some clothes and said it was a good time to make a mess of food.

"Dean, just leave your clothes outside the door I'll hang them up to dry down in the lobby." Then she left.

I told him the whole story about the case and most of what I knew except about the gold mine and the fact it was out there and June was working it.

"I wasn't going to tell you till later but you're here now so I can't hide it from you anymore. Just remember that if any of this gets out we might get dead right fast. You never know who to trust." June was standing in the doorway.

"I think we can trust Dean, Jim."

Dean looked up and June was in a pretty little dress with lace around the collar and down the front with a bow tied at her small waist. I never seen her look like this, then I looked over at Dean and he had a faraway look in his eyes and his gun he had been cleaning fell out of his hand to the floor. I bent over and picked it up and put it back in his hand.

"Dean, you better finish cleaning your gun you might need it."

"Okay, Jim I will." He said as he snapped out of his dream world."

"Come on you two I have supper on. We'll eat in the dining room tonight. I don't think those two will be back any time soon."

We sat and talked and the two of them sounded like they had known each other for years instead of a few hours. I knew what was going on but we had to get back to business cause this was a case of murder and one of us or all of us could be killed.

"Now, listen to me you two. I said listen." I yelled.

They both shut up and turned to me.

"Dean, June I can see that you two are getting along fine but we have a serious situation around here. We have a murderer to find and you both need to get your heads straight for now. June you need to get back to your old self of being careful all the time. After this you two will have your whole life to get to know about each other. I just want to add that June you are so beautiful but now isn't the time. I'm sorry to bust up a great night like this."

"Thank you Jim, I'm sorry I just hadn't been like a women in so long and now I have two good men friends that I can trust. It just went to my head. I'll be back to normal tomorrow."

"I'm sorry to Jim I know how important this case is to you two."

"Well, I understand you are both young and this case is important to all three of us now."

Dean and me went to our rooms and June went to where ever her room was. The next morning there was a large breakfast for us waiting in the dining room and then June came in dressed back in her old mining clothes with her old hat pulled down. We ate and we were kind of quiet when I said.

"Good to have the old June back."

"Well, I like the new and the old June myself." Dean said. That put a smile on her face.

"Jim, should I tell you where I live so you can find me easier."

"No June, leave it like it is for now. I don't want any slip ups and get you deeper in trouble."

Dean and me mounted up and left town and I was heading toward the mountains where Chance had been a few days ago. We stopped at noon and cooked up some grub on a small fire so not to attract anybody's attention. The mountains were right in front of us so we headed up to the ridge to have a look see.

"You know Jim, you haven't said two words all day."

"Sorry, just concentrating and I'm not use to having anyone with me except Red and he don't talk back much."

I looked out over the canyon but didn't see much so we went back down and I looked for tracks but none were found. We went into two more canyons with no luck.

"What are you looking for in all these canyons?"

"Tracks of some horses that may belong to those two that were in Marfa the other night. I saw the old tracks in the canyon where I saw them before. But nothing new so they must have been scared clear back to Alpine. I'm sure they'll be back but for now we'll head back to the ranch and help Gary get ready for the shearing of the sheep. I'll go into town at night and try to get any lead I can to go on."

"What are they looking for?"

"For June, they think she knows where her grandpa's so called gold mine is and they mean to make her tell. That's why I yelled at both of you last night. She needs to keep her head straight."

"You think she likes me."

"Boy, anybody except a blind man could see that you both liked each other. But you need to get your head out of the clouds for now."

"You think that there is a gold mine."

"I don't know for sure but I think it might just have been a way to try to keep people from leaving town. We'll bed down tonight and head to the ranch in the morning."

We rode in about noon and knew where Pickin's should be so we went right to work. There he was with our two dogs closing the gate as the herd went in the pasture.

"Where you boys been? Been doing all your work and mine."

"Been working west of here that Gary's thinkin' about gettin'."

"Guess you missed us?" Dean said.

"I wouldn't go as far as that, been nice gettin' a full night sleep and no outlaws to keep track of. Been like heaven at night. Now that y'all are back I better get used to being awake at night."

"Not this time we came to work. Got to get ready for the shearing."

"You might talk to Gary about that. The shearing barn sure could use a cleaning and get it ready."

We rode in at the end of the day and Gary was already on the porch.

"Glad to see you two. Catch anymore bad men."

"Not yet we came back to help to get ready for the shearing. Pickin's says the barn needs some cleaning out and setting up."

"Come on in and we'll have a talk about it. We been kind of shorthanded since Joe is in jail."

After dinner I went to town and Dean stayed and talked to Gary and Slim about cleaning and how to set up the barn for the sheep to come in and go down the line being sheared.

As I rode to town I went around a about way and came in from the east. I walked into the Long Bar and there were Chance and Fred sitting at a table. Then I saw Lola sitting with Ted in a corner. I got a beer and went to sit at another table when Ted called to me. I walked over and took a seat.

6

I didn't like it but I had to set with my back to Fred. I knew he was wanted for murder and I'm sure he wouldn't hesitate to shoot someone in the back.

Lola spoke, "Where you been? Haven't seen you in here lately."

"Gary sent me out west of here there's some canyon's with some good grass and water. He's thinking 'bout buying some more land now that the thieves are dead or in jail. Anything new around town."

Ted said, "You know years ago there was an old man claim there was gold in those mountains out west of here."

"You don't say. Never heard that myself. All I saw was an old ghost town that I spend one night in. Didn't see nobody."

"Well, I heard tell that he died some time back. I used to talk to him over there before the railroad came this way and everyone moved here."

That's when I felt a gun in my back and a click of a trigger. I put up my hands and turned around and there stood Fred.

"What's going on Fred?"

"Don't like anyone treating me like you did the other night."

"I'm sorry if I hurt your feeling but I had an appointment to keep. You sure look like you've seen a ghost."

I could see the shock in his eyes and how his hand became unsteady so I moved fast and grabbed the barrel and push it down as his gun went off and the bullet smashed into the floor. My knee came up as he lost his balance and it caught him right on the chin and he went down on his back. He was up with his gun still in his hand and as he pointed it at me again I jumped to his left side as he fired again. The bullet hit the table right in front of Ted and Ted jumped down to the floor as the bullet ricocheted and hit right above Lola's pretty little head into the wall. I grabbed his wrist and twisted it up above his head and back behind his back and the gun fell loose and hit the floor by Ted on the floor. I turned Fred and hit him straight in the face and he went flying but landed on his feet and grabbed a chair and threw it at me and I ducked as I heard a gun go off. I saw Fred come up on his toes and a blood spot was on the front of his shirt. I turned and Ted was dropping Fred's gun to the floor. About then the bat-winged doors flew open and John came in as I reached and picked up the gun off the floor. John looked at Fred dead on the floor and the surprised look on Ted's face and came over to me.

"I'll take that Jim. What happened here?"

I told him the whole story.

"Now, I can't say if Ted meant to shoot me or Fred. But I'd say he was protecting me John."

"Well, then I guess it's over. You two men over there get this dead body out of here and over to the undertakers."

I whispered to John, "You might check, that man was wanted for murder by the Rangers. Let them know he's dead."

John left and I picked up my hat and walked over to the table where Ted was.

"I hope you didn't mean that for me Ted."

"No, that's the first man I ever killed. I really didn't know what I was doing I just pulled the trigger. But thank you for keeping me from going to jail."

Lola came over and started right in, just like a woman. Bossy,

"Sit down let me clean your face up. Ted, bring a pan of water and a cloth."

As she was bathing my face I looked over and Chance was just sitting over at the same table playing solitaire.

"Sorry your friend had to die Chance."

"He wasn't a friend of mine just worked for me. His kind is a dime a dozen. I'll have another one here in three days."

"Well you better tell the next one to mind his own business."

He just waved his hand at me as to say, "so be".

"Thanks Lola but I better get back to the ranch."

I stopped by the sheriff's office.

"John, when you contact the Captain would you let him know what has happened and I'm fine. Tell him the case should be wrapped up in a few weeks."

"Sure thing Jim, why didn't you tell me about Fred."

"Thought he might be evolved in this case."

"Alright, but next time let me know what's going on. We are on the same side."

The next morning there was Pickin's and Dean looking at me when I woke up.

"Jim, what happened to you? You look terrible I hope the other man looks worst."

"He does, he's dead. I'll tell you about it later."

I washed my face and looked in the mirror. These are the days I really hate this job. I had to relive the whole thing over breakfast and Sara was taking swings at the air as I was telling what happened. Then Dean and me were in the shearing barn raking it out and moving things around. Then sitting up five stations for each man to grab a sheep and a pair of shears to cut the wool off without cutting them. The rams were most important not to cut cause one cut in the wrong place would mean no more lambs from that ewe. We finished by the end of the day and Gary was pleased with what we had accomplished in a day. After dinner I went to the bunkhouse and took off my boots and gun belt and just fell in my bunk. It was morning before I knew it and this morning I was up before Dean or Pickin's. I was sitting staring at them when they came to.

"How come you two slept so late?"

"What you mean late the sun's not even up? Go back to bed."

"We have things to do and places to go."

"What places?" Pickin's said.

We got going and ate and were out on the range by sunup. The sheep were doing great and their wool looked some of the best according to Pickin's. I just took his word for it. Dean rode over.

"Don't you think we should go and check on June? You know I don't even know her last name. Seems like I known her for years."

"Don't worry about June. She's been takin' care of herself for years and her grandfather to when he was alive. Her last name is Grayson. Now quite worrying about her and you know I don't know your last name."

"It's Gibbs."

"Now, what are you going to do about the case?"

"I've been thinking on that. I think I know who's involved but with the law you can't just go and accuse someone. You need to find evidence or catch them in the act, like the cattle and sheep stealing, in this case the deed had already happened. So that means we need evidence or if they took June and tried to get her to tell where the gold mine is and we caught them. If there's no gold mine June couldn't tell them anything in less she made it up and just led them to an old mine then she would really be in danger unless we were there to catch them red-handed."

"Don't even think about putting her life in danger. I wouldn't stand for it."

"Look Dean I understand how you feel and I wouldn't want to take a chance with her life. You have to realize that her life is in danger from now on if I don't catch them. They might get a hold of her one-day with me not around. I only would suggest that to her if there is no other way. It is up to her cause she has been hiding for a long spell now."

We worked the rest of the day and went in for dinner. I saw Sara walking to the barn as we rode up.

"Hello Sara, how is Sleeper doing?"

"She getting close I think, she seems to stay close to the barn."

"You know she might try to hide cause she thinks something might get her pups."

"I know, when she does go out I follow her and see where she goes. I try not to let her know."

"You keep up the good work cause her pups will be good sheep dogs if Gamer's the father he just won't give up."

After supper Dean and me rode to town. I didn't know what else to do just had to keep trying to get some more information out of Lola, Ted or Chance. I just hoped that nothing happens like the last time I came to town. As we rode into town John waved us down.

"Jim, just wanted to let you know there was a reward on Fred. I just don't know how I missed him in my posters. I looked again and there he was as big as life. Anyway who gets the reward?"

"Why, Ted, he shot him. By accident or not he got him."

"Alright, and the other matter they said to keep on and get it done. He would like some detail when possible. Jim, here is the thousand dollar reward I think you might want to see Ted's reaction. One more thing Lola and Chance rode out of town late last night and haven't been back. She was dressed for the trail, pants and gun belt and there's a new face in town so watch your back this time I checked close and he's not wanted."

"That might be interesting. See you later John, thanks."

"Wait I nearly forgot the trial for Joe and Shorty will be Monday a week from next would you tell Gary and Tom they might want to be there and might have to testify."

We tied up in front of the Long Bar and went inside. Ted was leaning on the bar. We walked up to the bar and I said out loud so everyone could hear. As I looked around there was a new face in town. "Hello Ted, just saw John and he gave me this for you."

"What he want giving me anything?"

"It's the thousand dollar reward for killing Fred."

The look on his face I will never forget like the face on a chicken when he sees the claws of a chicken hawk reach out to get him. I glanced over at the new face and he had a look of surprise all across his scarred face.

"You be quiet about that. I don't want any credit for that. You know I was just lucky. I don't want the reward." Ted whispered as I handed him the envelope.

Dean spoke up. "If it would had been me I would be downright glad to get that thousand dollars and take the credit. That was a bad dude. If you don't want it you can give it back to John."

"I would be glad of the reward to Dean, but I would hate to know what will happen when his friends find out he's dead and who killed him."

"Ted, where did Lola and Chance get off to."

"I don't know maybe a romantic weekend."

"Good luck, Ted."

We got our beers and sat down at the table by the new man in town. We really talked it up for on purpose for the new man.

"It sure would be nice to have that reward money."

"I don't know if you would live to spend it."

"You may be right, may not be worth it."

That's when the new man came over and leaned on our table and asked.

"What was this Fred's last name?"

"Who are you and why is it important to you?"

"I'm Lance Barlow, and I was going to meet a Fred Ward here for maybe a job."

"Well, mister you may need to look for another job unless you know who the job was with."

"You mean that tinhorn killed Fred Ward."

"Sure did, I was right here. Fred and me had a little disagreement cause his employer didn't like me getting out of a poker game that I was winning at the night before. It was just a nice clean fist fight when Fred pulled his gun and I knocked it out of his hand after his gun went off and nearly hit Ted. Ted picked up the gun and fired as I was ducking and the bullet ended up in Fred. Like I told the sheriff I didn't know if he was protecting me or shooting at my back. The sheriff gave him the benefit of the doubt and he got the reward."

"You say you know his employer?"

"Sure do, but he's not here seems he went out of town with a lovely little lady that works here."

"Thanks, what's the man's name?"

"Whose name?"

"Why his employer are you trying to get smart with me? Which way did they go?"

"Why no, I'm just an old sheep herder. Chance Larson, yelp that's the name. They probably went west not much east."

He left out the door and mounted and was out of town heading west.

"Let's go Dean, we can find where Lola and Chance went by following Lance."

"They left a day ago and there are lots of tracks."

"That's true but not two together with one riding a lot lighter in the saddle. Why should we do all the hard work?"

We gave him fifteen minutes or so and then headed west out of town toward the ranch and also toward Marfa. The two had now been gone more than a day. I found Lance's tracks as easy as pie and then I would see the two horses he was following. When we got well pass the road leading to the ranch there were a lot less tracks so we went into a gallop for I had an idea of one or two places where they would be heading and one of those places I was not too happy with. June might tend to trust a woman. That may be their thinking. When we came to the first cut off to a canyon the tracks kept on. I knew that there were at least twenty canyons around Marfa.

"I don't know Dean, there was the main trail to Marfa and the man is still on their tail."

We went on for another fifteen minutes and we saw a fire up ahead so we stopped and walked our horses and then we tied them to an old tall barrel cactus well off the trail and made our way to where my telescope could make out the area around the fire. Lance had found the two there and they were talking around the fire then I saw Lola get her blanket and lay down close to the fire for the nights out here in the desert were down right chilly. I told Dean.

"We might head back to the horses and get some sleep. I don't think they're going anywhere till morning."

Heading back I realized that it was really cold and we were going to have to do without a fire. We unsaddled the horses and got our bedrolls laid out and curled up and went to sleep. By the morning it was downright cold so I built a small fire and started coffee. I always carry coffee with a pot and some dry jerky. It wasn't much but it would keep us alive for a few days. Then Dean said.

"We should have went back to Marfa and slept in that nice warm hotel. We could have picked up their trail again today."

"And what if they would have found something while we were catching up to them today. Let's get on their trail right now."

We packed what little we had and headed in their direction. We moved up slow and with my telescope I could see that they were long gone. By the time we reached where they spend the night the fire was cold, they had left well before sunup. Sure enough there were three sets of tracks heading southwest. It seemed that they knew where they were headed. Dean said.

"I hadn't been this far west."

"I have but not this far south. I just wonder where they're heading and what their plan is. If they keep this way they will be in Mexico before noon."

"Can you go in Mexico?"

"I'm not supposed to but I will. I have to follow where this case might led."

By noon we were in Mexico and they turned straight south.

"There is a little village soon if they go pass it we'll stop and eat and buy some supplies. This might be a long trek. I know Gary needs our help but this is my job."

Their trail turned more east before reaching the village so we went on into the cantina. We ordered food with the little Spanish I knew and got a lot of rice and beans with eggs mixed in and some great tortillas and some beer. We filled up our canteens and went to a little store and got enough food for a week and some pans. The people were very friendly and grateful for the money. On the way out of the village a young man came running up and said.

"Senor, are you following someone. If you are there are soldiers to the south. There is a bigger village east that they may go to. There one can hire almost anything done."

"Thank you son that will be a great help." I tried to pay him a little.

"No thank you, the money you spent will help our village survived another winter. We don't need much. We are poor but we are proud."

Night fell before we got them in our sights but after dark we spotted a large fire.

"They sure don't care who sees them. Let's go back a ways so we can start a small fire behind some kind of barrier so they can't spot our fire."

We found some boulders and got a small fire going and ate supper. Dean said.

"You know where they're going?"

"I'm not for sure could be one of two places. It could be San Juan or maybe San Luis. San Luis is further but I understand that you can get almost anything you want done by hiring it done there. We have to be very careful down here. If someone asks you something just say, "me no understand" and let me handle it and keep your hands away from your gun unless they are fixin' to shoot. I never ask you how fast are you with that pistol."

"Fine with me. I never got hold of that lingo even living as close as we do to the border. I'm fair to middlin' with this here pistol."

In the morning we were up before the sun and they were gone just as fast. They still weren't trying to hide their trail so we stayed well behind them. They passed the road that led south to San Juan.

"See Dean they're going on to San Luis that was the road to San Juan."

We kept on their trail all day and camped outside of San Luis. Their trail led right into town but we couldn't take a chance to go in cause they would surly see us. It was a small town and when this many gringos show up at one time word would spread fast. We would go in after they left and find out what they did in the village. It wouldn't take much investigation to find out, for money will find out anything in San Luis. We built a fire behind a mound; it couldn't be call a hill, more of a large anthill.

"We'll get closer later tonight and try to see what they're doing."

"What you think they're doing?"

"I don't have much of a clue but you can bet it has to do with June. Now I'm pretty sure these three are involved in June's grandfather murder. I don't know about Ted or that drunk banker Sid Whasworth."

It was well after dark when we got close enough to town to be able to see with my telescope what was going on. This was a very rough town and we had to be very careful cause they were bound to have lookouts posted to kept an eye out for the federales. Now I could see in the cantina and there were Chance, Lola, Lance and a fourth man. As I zoomed in why it was Bud Timas. What? And where did he come from?

"Look Dean." I handed him the telescope and he eyed what was going on.

"See that fourth man at the table. That's Bud Timas he was in the canyon with Chance and Shorty. He must have already been here but why."

Dean handed the telescope back to me and I saw a girl dancing around the table and she took off her top and danced bare breasted close to the table and Lance reached out to grab her and she pushed him away. Then Bud reached for her and the same happened. Then the girl reached for Lola and the men in the cantina went wild and yelling. We could hear them from where we were, and she took Lola to the center of the floor and there she took off Lola's hat and started undoing her shirt and that set the men off again even the men around her table. When Lola was naked to the waist the two of them danced around in circles and then she led Lola to a back room with her arm draped around Lola shoulder with her hand on her breast. The men in the place clapped. Then another man came to the table and set. He looked very much like an Indian and Bud acted like he knew him. They talked for fifteen minutes and he got up and left out the back door. I could not make out where he went.

"Dean, I think we have seen enough for tonight."

We made our way back to the horses and then to camp. I put out the fire and we went to sleep. In the morning I laid there and thought of what they wanted with an Indian then it came to me, a tracker! I knew that June was good at hiding but I didn't think she was good enough to hide from an Indian tracker. I got a fire red hot but small and the smell of coffee and eggs and bacon got Dean up and going. We headed toward the village and as we got closer I saw two out riders and they rode up fast with their rifles laying over their saddles and fingers on the triggers. They motioned for us to head to town in front of them. I just hoped that our bunch was already gone. As we got closer I could see that their horses were gone from where they had been last night. As we rode up the street men came out from the buildings on both sides of the street. Then we were in front of the cantina and a man came out with no shirt on and wearing a large sombrero with a big smile on his face under his mustache and the still half naked girl from last night was by his side holding on to him.

"Si, who do we have here?"

"I'm Jim and this is Dean. I'm glad you speak English cause my Mexican is really poor."

"Jim what?"

"Jim Taylor from up El Paso way. Dean here works for me."

"What you want in my little village?"

I had to think fast, I knew a Mexican ranch a little northeast of here. I had to take a chance.

"We seemed to had gotten turn around I think we went too far west. We were on our way to the hacienda of Louis Garcia. I was going to see about buying some horses. I understand he has some of the finest in all of Mexico."

"This is true but I know of no one he is expecting. And I never see a white man come across the border to buy horses they usually come to steal."

"Senor, could we talk in the shade or even better have a beer in the cantina."

"Senor, I am sorry this is so rued of me. Let us go inside."

We walked inside and sat at a table and I said.

"Me steal, look I know better than to come to steal horses with just one man. This is true. You haven't said your name but I'll buy a beer for you any way and your lovely friend here."

He motioned to the man at the bar. Here came our beer and two plates of food. He laughed.

"My name is Juan Gómez and this is not a friend of mine this is just a young whore that comes around. You should have seen her last night a lady of your kind was here and Rosa stripped her naked right here and took her to bed and I watched awhile then I join the two of them. Much fun."

"I bet, what was a lone white woman doing here alone?"

"She not alone, had some men friends with her. They did not seem to mind her spending the night with us. But what could they do about it. Right Rosa." He said as he squeezed her naked breast.

We finished our food and beers and paid for everything.

"We better get going now we have some horses to see."

"Wait, you can't leave. You need to take some pleasure with Rose."

"Believe me I would but we have to be back at our ranch in two days and we're a day and a half late already. If we don't show up on time my wife will send all fifty of my men down here to find me. So I'll have to lose out on that pleasure. You know how wife's are."

Juan laughed. I know my wife tries to keep me at her place but I rather be here with this young one."

He waved to his men and they parted the way, for they had been around us like a fence keeping us in ever since we came into town, and Dean and me went out in the bright sun and mounted up and we were out of town to the northeast.

"Dean, don't look back. You don't know how close that was. If he didn't have his mind on that young woman we might not had got out of there so easy."

"The way they first looked at us I thought we were dead and buried."

"We have to locate Lola's tracks again and find out what they're up to."

Crisscrossing for some time and going in the same direction finally paid off.

"Look, here are their tracks heading north. They are going at a fair pace but they were three and now they're five and with Lola not getting any sleep last night they will be slowing down at her insistence. I now believe she might be the mind behind all of June's trouble."

Sure enough they started to slow down and soon there were only four sets of tracks.

"Dean, the Indian has left them but heading in the same direction. Get an eyeball full of that track. It's the Indian's tracks and we can follow him till he discovers someone is on his back trail. They must have told him where to search."

We found where they had stopped just awhile before so we gave them a wide berth and found the Indian's trail again.

"Dean, now keep an eye on our back trail in case they get energized. It's almost dark and he's still going that means that he doesn't have any kind of trail yet cause he may be good but he can't track in the dark. If there's a full moon he might be able to."

After dark we camped about half a mile off the trail we ate and bedded down for the night. There wasn't a full moon so I sleep peaceable. In the morning we had to eat jerky and do without coffee and we were gone before sunup. Two hours we came to where he had camped the night before. I could barely tell where he had cooked and slept. The day was hot and the sweat was rolling off both of us as we made our way to the northeast and closer to Marfa. About noon we came to the cut off that lead to Marfa but the Indian kept to the same trail. He was heading to the canyons to try to find the mine or any sign of June. When we came to the trail to Alpine I took it. I had an idea and we had to get to Alpine.

"Where are we going?"

"We have an appointment with a banker and a saloon keeper."

"What about June?"

"She can take care of herself. I told you that. When I first went in Marfa I couldn't find any evident of anyone being there except everything was clean but I couldn't find any tracks leading in or out of town. I'm a better than good tracker and that Indian is probably better than me but I don't think he can find her or her mine."

By nightfall we were still a ways from town so we camped and built a fire and ate a good supper. I had some oats with us so I gave some to the horses and hobbled them in a nice patch of grass and a creek nearby. By morning the horses were raring to go and we didn't disappoint them. It was ten o'clock in the morning when we rode up the street and tied up in front of the Long Bar. It was still too early for Ted but the bank was open. We headed that way. We walked up to the teller and I asked.

"We would like to see Mr. Whasworth."

"May I ask your business?"

"Just tell him it has to do with a case of murder and his lively hood."

He went in the office behind the teller cages and knocked on the door. The door opened and Sid looked at us and went back inside and the teller came out."

"I regret to inform you that he is busy for the rest of the day."

"Oh, I think not."

I pushed open the gate to the back and went to the door and knocked. The teller tried to bar our way but we pushed by him and I turned the doorknob and we entered a small room with Sid Whasworth sitting behind a very large desk.

7

"What's the meaning of this? I said I was busy all day."
"To busy to keep yourself out of jail or from being hanged."

"What do you mean jail or be hanged? I have not done anything and who are you any way. I'll have nothing to say to you."

"I'll be talking to Ted later today and see what he has to say about the situation and then to John. Wait until you see him mad."

"I did nothing wrong."

"We know about what was going on with the ranches and I don't know what the banking examiner will think about all of this but we'll find out."

We turned and paraded out of the office and straight out the front door to our horses. We went in the alley beside the general store and waited. In half an hour Sid came out and he was looking all up and down the street as he entered John's office. He spent awhile in there then came out to the general store and then to the livery and last to the Long Bar. Then men from the livery and the general store went in the Long Bar. Then to my amazement John went to the Long Bar.

"What you make of that Dean?"

"Hard to say. But if Sid complained about us why did John go to meet with the others and not come to find us right away before we might have left town?"

"Who owns the general store and the livery?"

"That would be Jeb Land he owns the livery and Todd Justin owns the general store."

"Did these four men live in Marfa before the railroad came to Alpine."

"That was before my time but I know the sheriff has been around for years. You know that Gary and Tom had their ranches for a long while before the railroad came. I know cause the men use to talk about having to drive the cattle to Lubbock and they would see the sheepherders takin' the wool in wagons to Lubbock. At one time they talked of setting fire to the wagons but Tom stopped them. Always said he wouldn't start trouble but he would stop it if trouble came his way."

"Why don't we take a ride?"

We made our way out of town and headed down the road to Tom's ranch. When we came in the yard Tom came out.

"What you doing over this way? Heard Gary going to be shearing in a couple of weeks."

"He is and I hope I can wrap up the case I'm working on before then. Dean said that you and Gary had your ranches before the railroad came to town."

"Sure did and we both use to go clean to Marfa to get supplies. Come to think of it we never had any trouble till everyone moved to Alpine."

"That's what I'm looking to find out. Did Sid in the bank and Jeb in the livery and Todd at the general store and how about John when did he come in the picture. I already know that Ted came from Marfa?"

"Well now, you're pushing my mind a ways back. You're right about Ted I use to get a beer in the saloon over there and would see him. Now Sid I knew cause I had to get a loan on the ranch in those days. I dealt with Todd to and now I remember Jeb cause that was before I could afford a blacksmith to be full time at the ranch and he shoed the horses and other odd jobs. Now seems to me that John was already sheriff in Alpine. Seems to me there was a sheriff in Marfa by the name of Jimmy Johnson. When the people moved to Alpine I just assumed that cause John was in Alpine that Jimmy just went to another town."

"Did you ever know an old prospector name of Guy Grayson?"

"You are pushing my mind to its limit. I tell you."

Just then the screen door opened and Tom's wife came out on the porch. Dean and me took off our hats.

"Morning, ma'am."

"Jim, this is my misses Betty. Dean you know Betty."

"Yes sir. How are you ma'am?"

"I'm good Dean, now Tom, you're not that old remember when you went to the saloon, which I didn't approve of at all, you said that there was a man that always was taking about finding gold in the mountains north of Marfa. You never told me his name but you thought he was crazy cause you were sure there was no gold anywhere around here."

"That seems right now, thank you dear."

"How about Lola? That works in the Long Bar in Alpine now?"

"Yes, Tom what about Lola."

"Now dear this is business."

"You two want to come in for dinner."

"You mean at the bunkhouse. No ma'am."

"No Dean I mean my cooking."

"Yes, ma'am. Come on Jim we haven't had a good meal since June fed us. We been losing weight eating our own cooking."

"It would be our pleasure."

"I told you Tom that cook of yours was running off the good men. I bet Bonnie cooks for Gary's men."

"She sure does and she's one of the best."

We ate and talked about the times when Marfa was a booming town. It seemed that Lola already owned the Long Bar with a partner besides Ted and Ted bought in later but Chance was in Marfa and then went back east till last week. Now I thought about how long it had been since we had a good meal my mind had forgotten but my stomach hadn't.

"Thank you Tom for the information and Betty it was sure a pleasure to eat at your table."

"Same goes for me ma'am." Dean said.

As we headed back to town to talk to Ted I heard Betty say.

"Now Tom we're going to have a talk about Lola."

As we rode up the street and tied up and then we went into the Long Bar there was Ted at one of the tables nursing a drink.

"Have a seat boys and have a drink on me?"

He waved for Doby to bring two beers. We sit there drinking our beers. Then Ted spoke out.

"From what I see you two are in a lot of trouble."

"How do you see that?"

"It seems that Sid went to tell John about you two busting into his office. Then we had a little meeting with the other councilmen and then all of us went about our business. But one thing I didn't understand before the meeting Sid was nervous and he was saying things like "we're going to get caught". And "I don't know how you could have done it."

"What happened at the meeting? That doesn't sound like we're in trouble."

"Well, that's not all. When John came he told us you're a Texas Ranger and we had nothing to worry about. Your investigation had nothing to do with anything around here so the meeting broke up. Then later, about noon Jeb found Sid out behind his livery with a hole in his back seems to have come from a pistol. But not from a little pistol like I carry it was a large size pistol and no one in town carries a pistol of the size that shot Sid."

"It wasn't us we weren't even in town." I said as I reached in my pocket and pinned my star on my vest."

"Well I'll be, I didn't know whether to believe John or not. I don't think you did it but the others seem to. I don't know if John does but he's looking for you two."

"I kind of like you Ted I hope you don't have anything to do with all this."

"I don't, whatever it is. No one has said but whatever it is, will get around town soon. Don't make a quick move John is coming in the door."

I told Dean, "Take it easy Dean, John's a dead shot. We'll get out of this."

I turned around and looked at John.

"Hello there John, Ted said that you might want to talk to us. We were just going to come to see you."

"That's fine, I think we can talk better in my office."

"Can we finish our beer?"

"Sure, just keep your hands away from your guns."

"You heard him Dean, just take it easy."

"Yes sir. I've no intention of getting shot if I can help it."

We walked to John's office and he closed the door behind us.

"What's going on John?"

John put his finger to his lip and said "Sha" then he stepped over and shut the door that led to the cells where Joe and Shorty were locked up.

"I had to make them think that I thought it might be one of you that killed Sid cause I think it's one of them. I saw how nervous Sid was and I saw you two leave town. Do you think this might have to do with your case?"

"I'm not for sure. My case is about a murder that happened over in Marfa a few months ago. I found out that Sid had loaned Ted money to buy into the saloon and Sid had loaned money to Tom and Gary on their ranches. Then right after that all the trouble started between Tom and Gary. I thought all three things might be connected so I was trying to get information out of Sid."

"It might be. Just watch yourself cause the two murders might also be connected."

John walked over and opened the door leading to the cells. He pointed to the cells and then to his ears.

"Jim, Dean I'm going to let you go for now but you stay around the area. I'll investigate more and get to the bottom of Sid's murder."

"Thanks John."

I gathered up Red's reins and jumped on his back and we were out of town with Dean trying to keep up.

"Where you going in such a hurry?"

"You forget about June that Indian is on her trail or trying to be."

"You're right, let's get going. Where you think that Indian is looking?"

"First we'll look around the canyons then we'll head over to Marfa if we have to. I think all their planning is going wrong or Sid wouldn't have been murder this morning."

"If that Indian is a good tracker how long can we get away with watching them?"

"That is a good question. We just have to hope it's long enough."

I found where the other three caught up with the Indian and they were somewhere near so we went to the rim of the canyon and sure enough they were in the bottom of an arroyo that was at the north end of the canyon. I could tell that they were talking to the Indian and then they would talk among themselves. Then the Indian left the canyon and I saw him stop and look our way then head to another canyon and the three would follow him like a little puppy. This went on all day and when it was just about sundown the four headed east toward Alpine. We camped about two miles from them. I hobbled our horses in a small grassy area close in. We had no fire so jerky had to do.

Dean said. "You know I'm getting tired of this I hope they make a move soon. One day we eat like kings at Tom's and the next we're stuck with eating this jerky and no coffee."

"Well, that's the life of a Ranger. We might as well turn in and get a good night sleep while we can."

I was trying to go to sleep but tonight sleep wouldn't come.

"You know Dean, today that Indian looked right our way. I think he saw our tracks."

But Dean didn't answer he was asleep. So I turned over with my gun in my hand and tried to sleep. Then about two in the morning Red snorted and I was awake but didn't make a move right away. I laid and listened and then turned slowly and threw off the blanket and was on my feet. I didn't have time to wake Dean so I laid back in the brush and got my eyes adjusted to the dark and then I heard a scrape on a rock and I moved quick to bend down and a knife came within an inch of my head. As I bent I saw a moccasin boot between my legs so I grabbed it and rose up and the Indian went flat on his back. He was up with his knife in his hand and came at me. I tripped him up with my boot and he went flying into the cactus. His knife fell out of his hand and he was still. That's when Dean woke up and I pulled the Indian up out of the cactus and he yelled as I threw him down on his back, cause of the cactus needles in his back. I got my rope and tied him up.

"Who is he?" Dean said.

"That's what we're going to find out right now. What is your name?"

He didn't speak so I pushed down on his stomach and the needles stuck him in the back. Then I let up.

"I asked, what is your name? I know you speak English I saw you talking to your friends."

"No friends of mine. Just do for money."

"What is your name? What you do for money?"

I pushed him down on his back again and he spoke.

"Name Big Tim I look for small tracks. Maybe a girl did not tell. All I know."

"Why you try to kill me."

"Thought you one look for Big Tim. Saw tracks outside canyon. Men want to kill. I not do what they say but do not believe Big Tim. That why in Mexico."

"I do not look for you. I'll let you up and untie you and pull the cactus out of your back if you promise not to try to kill me."

"Give my word. Big Tim is honest. No want trouble."

"You trust him." Dean said.

"I do. Most Indians you can trust if they give their word."

I let him loose and I started pulling the cactus needles out of his back. I could tell it pained him but he didn't let out a sound. I pulled them all out and he took off his shirt so I could put some suave on his back that's when I could see the rippling muscles on his back and when he stood up he was a good three inches above me and I'm 6'2". I'm just glad that fight didn't last long or I would have been in real trouble.

"Big Tim, how much were they paying you?"

"A hundred dollars. Send to wife for her and my children in Arizona."

"I watch these people you are with; I think they are bad people. I think you are good. I will give you the hundred dollars to send to your wife if you leave in the morning and do not help them."

"Think I will go home I am lonely for my family. Will try to make men know that I did not do what they say I do."

"I will give you a letter for you to give to those men. I am a Texas Ranger and I'll tell them what good you did for me and to listen to your side. It may help I don't know. You will just have to hope it will or take your family and start off fresh."

Then Dean said, "Write me Dean Gibbs in Alpine and you can come here. I will help you. I bet you know about sheep."

"Thank you, I know much about sheep. Glad I did not kill."

"Big Tim, I am also glad."

We laughed and Big Tim brought in his horse and we went back to sleep. In the morning I gave him the letter and some food and the money and as he went Dean said.

"Tell you what to tell them; I find no tracks if someone doing something to them it must be a ghost. I not like ghost."

"Hope to see you soon."

We turned our attention back to the other three. They were still heading toward Alpine and their camp looked as if they were confused with the desertion of the Indian. We trailed them back to Alpine. We turned down the trail to Gary's ranch.

Sara was out in the yard when we rode up and Bonnie came out.

Sara said, "We heard about you being a Texas Ranger at the trial. I knew you weren't no sheep man but you're great in my book."

"Thanks Sara, that means a lot. Bonnie what happened to Joe and Shorty."

"They will hang Shorty and Joe got five years. Here comes Gary the men are never late for dinner. You and Dean will eat here."

Gary got down and shook our hands.

"I invited them to dinner, Gary."

"Sure, after what you two did for Tom and me you two are invited any time and you can stay in the bunkhouse any time."

We sat and ate and the conversation turned to my case.

"You know that Sid was killed yesterday."

"We heard, how is your case coming?"

"I have a led or two. Do you know anything about Chance, Jeb, Todd or what happened to Jimmy Johnson the sheriff of Marfa or even Lola? If I knew more it could be of help."

"I know they all came from Marfa except Lola and John they were both here before the railroad came. Let me remember Todd came to town with about three wagons loaded with the merchandise from his store in Marfa. Chance was just a gambler but he left about two weeks later I think he went back east it was said. Now Jeb came to town with not much or nothing at all maybe his horse and some clothes. He had the livery over in Marfa but I don't know what happened but I know he came with nothing. Everyone assumed that he got a loan from Sid. Now Sid came with money but that was enough to start a bank. I always thought that the bank suited him cause he was always nervous."

"That helps a little. I came by to let you know that when you get ready to shear the sheep we'll be here. I wouldn't think of leaving you shorthanded."

"That will be a help. I'll send for you a day or two before so we can show you how to use the shears."

"You know Gary I think we'll stay here tonight I need time to think and ask Dean he's tried of sleeping under the stars."

"It's not so much that, it's not eatin' a good meal once in a while."

Bonnie added. "You won't have that problem around here."

"Just sign me up for a night in this luxury hotel." Dean said.

It was nice to sleep in a bed and Dean was out like a baby but I lay there thinking. Lola and Chance or Ted could have killed Guy but Lola and Chance were not in town when Sid was killed. So that left Ted, Jeb or Todd that could have killed Sid. Where did Lance come in, was he just a hired gun. Jeb came to town with not much and Sid had money. So where did he get his money and where did Jeb get the money to start the livery. It was a puzzle that was waiting to be solved. On top of that everyone now knew I am a Texas Ranger. So I went ahead and pinned on my badge.

The next morning I headed to town by myself and left Dean to help Gary get ready for the shearing. As I rode up the street I noticed that they were building the gallows to hang Shorty in the middle of town. I went to the sheriff's office and put on my badge. I knew that after the trial everyone in town knew who I was even Lola and Chance. When I walked in John wasn't there so I went in to talk to Shorty. He was lying on the bed like he had not a care in the world.

"Shorty, I need to talk to you."

"Go ahead and talk can't do me no more harm. But don't expect an answer out of me. I told Bart you was some kind of badge. He just never listened."

"Were you working for someone beside Bart?"

"Can't say. Except Tom's, running his cattle."

"You know anything about a killing over in Marfa about four months ago an old prospector?"

"Nope, my minds a blank."

"I hope you have fun dangling from the end of the rope tomorrow morning."

"I know someone will get me out of here before then."

"Who!"

"Never you mind."

Then Joe spoke up out of the corner of the other cell.

"Jim, you're talking to the wrong man. If you can get my sentence reduced I can tell you a little. I never meant to hurt anyone it was just about the money."

"I don't know Joe, I could try but I couldn't promise you anything, that's up to the judge."

"You shut your mouth. I'll get you or someone will. I told Bart not to trust you."

"Shorty, you seem so smart. Tell me how come you're hanging tomorrow."

"You shut-up you law boy. You'll get yours one day."

"Go ahead Joe."

"When we were out takin' the cattle Shorty and Bart would go out a ways from the fire at night. I know there were two other people and I could hear some of what they said but not all and I never seen them."

"Did you recognize their voice or anything else about them or anything they said?"

"I never thought about it that way."

"That's not much to go on. You think on it and I'll come back tomorrow. I'll see what I can do with the judge."

That's when John came in.

"What you doing in there Jim?"

"Just trying to get some information out of them before they're gone."

"Any luck. They won't talk to me about what when on. Sure nothing about the murders of Sid or the old prospector in Marfa."

"I'll just have to keep looking. See you later if you don't mind I'll come talk to Joe before he leaves for Austin."

"Sure thing, any time."

I led Red over to the hitching rail in front of the Long Bar. I might as well face Chance and Lola I was thinking when I walked through the bat-winged doors. Lola and Chance were sitting at a table with Ted. I didn't see Lance anywhere and that was a little concerning but I could handle him. I walked over to the table and pulled out a chair and sat down with my back facing the wall.

"Hello Lola, Chance. Where you been the last few days on a romantic holiday?

Lola spoke up first. "I don't know if I want to talk to you. You should had made me aware that you were a Ranger."

"I didn't know it mattered to you what I was and we don't advertise much."

Then Chance chimed in. "I didn't know the Texas Rangers let you take money away from an honest person."

"Well, Chance I was on my own time and I could see the game you were playing let me win some and sucker me in and then deal me the bad hands till you had all your money back and all my money besides with your marked deck of cards."

"Why I never did any such thing."

Ted was laughing. "Chance, look like he got the best of you."

"You be quiet Ted."

"I could have arrested you and you would be in jail right now. Maybe that would suit you it would give you time to talk to Shorty before tomorrow morning."

"I don't know what you mean. I don't know Shorty."

That's when I saw Lance come in the door and he looked mad. He came over to the table. He looked me straight in the eyes.

"I don't like any Texas Ranger, especially one that got my friend killed."

"Now Lance, you don't want to mess with Jim. He didn't kill Fred you know Ted accidently shot him." Chance said.

"Yea, but he was the cause of Fred dying."

"Son, look at it from my point of view. I think you're too young to die and I don't want to be the one to kill you."

Lola put in. "Lance, you don't know how fast he is."

"I don't care, I'm going to kill you."

"You better talk some sense into your boy Chance or you're going to have to find you other boy."

"He's on his own, I don't want any part of this. Jim, I'd nothing to do with this."

I had to make up my mind whether to wound him or killed him. He would come after me again if I wounded him. I kept a watch on his eyes. Everyone around us moved to a safe distant away. They could see now I was through talking. I was going to try one more thing.

"I guess you're right the time to back away has long passed. Do what you have to kid. I hope you can take a last breath before you die."

His eyes moved ever the slightest and his hand was on the butt of his gun and was starting to come out of his holster and mine was already even with him and my thumb had the hammer back already and my forefinger was on the trigger as his was coming even with me. Then as I pulled the trigger I could see the astonished look in his eyes as the bullet went straight into his body. He pulled the trigger as he fell to the floor and his bullet when into the floor by the table leg. Lola went to him and bent down and I could hear him say.

"I can't believe he beat me."

Then Lance died right there on the floor of the Long Bar saloon at the age of twenty-two. John came rushing in and looked the situation over.

"Is this what it looks to be."

"Yes, if it look to you that he tried to out draw me. It is."

Ted spoke up. "John, the kid came in looking to kill Jim. Jim gave him ever chance to back out and he wouldn't. He got the chance he wanted."

"Then boys take him away."

Then John left and I put my gun back in my holster. This was part of the job that I never got use too. As I left I could hear the men starting to talk as I mounted Red and headed to the ranch. The day was bright and sunny with not a cloud in the sky a nice summer day. But this made not a difference to me it felt like a dark, cloudy winter day. I took my time riding back for I never knew how to tell anyone that I killed someone. Of course I would not say anything but they would ask what happened in town and I would have to say, it was my way.

8

Then came a shot from a rifle and Red took a roll on his side and I was out of the saddle and behind a boulder close to the road. I looked and Red was still down as I searched the hills around me. But nothing gave me a target to shoot at. Then I saw a flash of sunlight off a barrel of a rifle as it disappeared behind a boulder a ways off. I kept my eyes glued to that spot and the area around it for a full five minutes but they must have gone. I went to Red to check on him for he was still down. I went over his body and legs and found nothing. Then around his ear I found a shallow crease made by the bullet and that's when he came too and tried to get up. I patted him on the head and rubbed my hand along his mane and his side as he made it to his feet.

"Take it easy boy. We'll get you back to the barn and take care of that. You'll be fine."

Red shook his head and we started walking toward the ranch. As we walked the dizziness seemed to be disappearing from Red. I was just about to mount and walk him slow when another bullet rang out and hit a stone by Reds feet. I rushed him behind three or four boulders. I took my rifle and telescope off Red and left him there and headed on foot up and around the many boulders scattered around the area. At the top of one boulder I held up the telescope and looked all over and saw nothing. Then I spotted him but I couldn't tell who it was but the clothes were of the kind in town not on a ranch. I kept working my way down the backside of where he was and when I was near him he made a move toward where I had left Red and I followed until he reached Red then he saw I wasn't there and started to turn and I hit him over the head. He went down and didn't get up. I got my rope and tied his hands behind his back and turned him over. But as I did his hat fell off and there was hair that fell down her back to her waist. She was dressed like a man with a coat and pants. She looked around twenty but I didn't recognize her but she must know who I was. I left her and went to look for her horse. I found her horse and when I got back she was awake and mad as a wet hen.

"What you mean hitting me like that?" She said as if she had done nothing wrong.

"You're lucky that I didn't kill you. You shot my horse and then came back and made another try."

"Well, you can untie me now."

"Not on your life. I take it very unfriendly when someone shoots at me. First I'm going to take you to Gary Thomas's ranch and take care of my horse. Then we're heading back to town for a jail cell for you. You can't go around shooting at people. Especially a Texas Ranger."

"I didn't know who you were."

"Then why did you come back to make sure you got the job done?"

I got her on her horse and I rode Red slow and in about an hour we reached the ranch and I headed to the barn. Everyone came a running as I got her off the horse and she tried to kick me.

"You keep that up and I'll tie your feet."

"Jim, what you got there, a wildcat." Gary said.

I took off Red's saddle and got some water and begun to wash his wound.

"This female tried to kill me and hit Red down the road apiece. She's lucky I didn't kill her. She's dressed like a man."

Then Bonnie and Sara came in the barn with Dean and Pickin's running behind them. I took off her hat and her hair tumbled down her back and I could see the look of amazement on everyone's face.

"Shelly, what you doing dressed like that and shooting at Jim? He's a Texas Ranger and he's working with us." Bonnie said.

"How was I to know that? I thought he was the one that shot at me earlier in the day. Made me fall off my horse and nearly broke my neck. It made me so mad that I went home and got my rifle and put on these clothes and headed to look for the hombre that shot at me. I'm sorry about your horse."

Bonnie said, "Jim, can you please untie her this is Tom's daughter."

"You sure, look what she did to Red. I was taking her to jail after I borrowed a horse."

I looked over and Sara was bathing Red's wound and left and came back with some ointment for the wound. Then I heard everyone laughing.

"I'm sure Jim."

I untied her and Bonnie took her to the house after Shelly reached and took her saddlebags with her.

"I just wonder who shot at her and why? You don't think someone is trying to start us fighting again." Gary said.

"I don't know what they would have to gain."

Then Dean said. "Jim, I've known her since I've been here and I'm sure she didn't mean to shoot Red. I've never known her to lie about anything."

Bonnie and Shelly came out of the house and she looked so different. She had a dress on with her hair all brushed out. She was beautiful and she walked right up to me and took my hand and looked me in the eyes.

"Jim, if I had known who you was I wouldn't have shot at you and I love horses. Red is so beautiful; I sure wouldn't had shot him. If you have to take me to jail then I won't resist you." Sara spoke to me.

"Jim, Red is all right it was just a scratch. It must have hit a little vein and it bleed a lot."

"I guess since Red is fine and you really were in danger and Tom is a good man. I'll let you go."

Then Bonnie said. "Now everyone come to dinner, you to Shelly. You can tell your mother that we hog tied you and made you eat with us."

Everyone was laughing as we walked to the house for dinner and Shelly seemed not to want to let go of my arm. My mind was working all the time we were eating. Shelly was beautiful but I still had a case to solve and who and why did someone shoot at her.

"Shelly, I've asked everyone else about Marfa before the railroad came to Alpine. Do you remember anything about those days?"

"How far back? When I was young there was a girl she was a little older than me and we played together when mother was in the store. Then when I was older I only saw her sometimes and we talked a little." "What did you talk about? Anything about her grandfather?"

"She always talked about how her and her grandfather went in the mountains and he was looking for silver or gold. Then when the people started moving over here I only saw her once more and that was here in Alpine and I tried to talk to her but she ran away. I ran after her and turned a corner then I noticed that there was an older man and John seem to be following her but then John went back to his office but the other man got on his horse and left town after she did. That's all I know. I never met her grandfather but the way she talked about him he sounded like a real likable man."

"How long ago did you see the man follow her out of town? Did you know him?"

"Oh, I guess about five years ago. I've never seen the man before until about a week ago and that was in the general store. He was buying some cards and cigars. At the time I thought he might work in the saloon but I've never been in there. I hope that helps. Bonnie I better get home the folks might be worried about me."

We walked out with her and she told me.

"I hope to see you again, Jim." Then she was off down the road.

In the morning Dean and me along with the men went to town so see Shorty hang. When we rode up the street I could see that it wasn't an ordinary day. There were so many people out in the street that it was troublesome to make our way down the street. The gallows was there in the middle of the square with people all around the bottom of the gallows that was at least twelve feet above the ground with stairs leading up to the platform. Then a beam went across the platform and that was attached to two poles coming up from the platform. A rope with a noose was attached to the beam going across. Then the platform had a door in it. Two men were testing the trap door with a lever on the railing that went around the whole platform. It seemed to work perfectly. I was going to John's office to talk to Joe again but now it was too late cause the sheriff and two deputies came out of the jail with Shorty in front of them with hands tied in back of him. As he started pass me I said.

"Where's your help? Anything you want to tell me."

"Nope, I guess my friend is busy, you'll have hell finding out anything. But I wish you luck."

They led him up the stairs and put the rope over his head and around his neck then a bag went over his head. One of the deputies pulled the lever and Shorty fell a short ways till he reach the end of his rope and it was over. I noticed as the deputies were taking away Shorty's body that John had gone back to his office. I started to the sheriff's office to talk to Joe with Dean beside me. Before we had taken ten steps toward the office we heard four shots come from the jail. As we rushed to the office I saw Gary and Pickin's and there were Slim and Bob coming up behind them. As we entered the office there was Joe lying on the floor with a gun in his hand outside of the jail cell and John was standing over him with his gun in his hand. He looked at us. "I came in the door and he was out of the cell and had a gun. He started to raise the gun and someone shot him in the back when I was about to shoot him."

"How did he get the gun?"

"I don't know unless someone passed it through the bars in the cell from the ally while we were busy with Shorty. The shot must have come from there."

"That makes sense. Look he's still alive."

I bent down and got close to Joe. I could tell he wasn't going to make it. He had blood coming out of his mouth. Joe whispered low near out of breath.

"Bart talked about one of the people and said he had a scar on the back of his neck, a deep scar, under where the collar is. Gun put in hand."

"What Joe? Joe, what did you say?"

"Woma!" He died.

"What did he say Jim?" John asked.

"I couldn't make it out."

I wasn't going to give away a good lead. That's when Tom came in the office and Shelly was with him. When she saw the body she turned her head and put a hand over her mouth. I took Shelly by the hand and led her outside.

"That's no place for a young lady."

"Thank you Jim, the hanging was bad enough but to walk in and see a dead man on the floor made this day even worse."

"I just never get use to the hangings either. I know they're necessary but they still bother me."

Tom and then Gary came out of the office with the rest of the men.

"Come Shelly let's get back to the ranch. See you later Gary."

"Dad, I'm so glad you and Gary are getting along so well now. I always had a fond feeling for all the Thomas family."

"Tom, Shelly told you what happened yesterday. I think you should keep a close watch on her."

"You don't think it was an accident."

"Shelly, think back about those two men and all that went on back then. You may have seen something that you weren't supposed to see.

"Why would they wait until now? I've been here for all these years."

"No one was investigating it till now and you might remember something that could expose them. I'll see you in a few days. Just think on it."

Gary left and the men and me went to have a beer. The Long Bar had been closed for the hanging but now it was doing a booming business. There was Ted and Chance sitting at a table over in the corner and Lola was just coming out of the office. Dean and me got a beer and sat at a table. Dean said.

"Joe said something didn't he? I saw your face."

"Yes, but I wasn't going to let the whole town know. He was murdered like Sid and Guy."

"What can we do?"

"This is a puzzling case and I'm still puzzled over who would want to kill Shelly. That could be a fourth."

"You think they would go after her again."

"If she might remember something."

Lola came over and took a seat at our table.

"I just heard that Joe was killed and that hanging was atrocious. Too bad I liked the both of them but they seemed to have gone bad."

"I've never seen you dance around here. You must dance some night with one of the other girls. I bet the men around here would like that."

"What do you mean?"

"Oh, nothing it was just a thought. I saw that happen one time in Mexico and just found it interesting. That's all."

"I don't think they would appreciate that kind of dance up here."

"Where did you and Chance spend your time away from here?"

"No where special. We're just friends and now I'll leave at that."

She left our table and went over to the table where Chance and Ted was. Ted got up and came over to us.

"What did you say to her? She was mad as I've ever seen her."

"Just asked her to dance with one of the girls."

"Don't know why that got her so hot. Have John or you found who killed Sid?"

"No, but I'm working on it. Heard you owed him on a loan. Who do you pay now?"

"I know what you're getting at but I didn't owe him enough to kill him for. I guess I'll pay it to his wife. I don't know."

"Ted, were Lola or Chance gone yesterday?"

"I was looking for Lola but I found her about an hour later and Chance I don't keep track of him. I don't know what got into that kid yesterday. I better get back before they beat each other to death."

"You nearly told her we were following her in Mexico. What kid?"

"I meant to. Just putting out some little barbs I want to see what sticks. Lance made a play for his gun and I had to shoot him. He just wouldn't give it up. I'm going to hang around and see if anything happens."

I left the Long Bar and lead Red around the corner of the corral and waited. Most of the cowhands and the sheep men left and the town was emptying out. The sun was in a hurry to go down in the west. Then Lola came out of the Long Bar and hurried down the street and went into an ally by a house I hadn't noticed before. I left Red and hurried behind the house and looked in the back window. There was Lola talking to a woman that I'd never had seen before. Then Todd came in the front door and they were arguing. I could make out that Lola was telling them that I had followed her to Mexico. Then they moved into the next room and I couldn't hear anything more. Lola came out and went over to the sheriff's house and knocked and John's wife let her in. From the back window I could see them but couldn't hear them. John wasn't home yet but these two seemed to be real good friends. That seemed unusual that a saloon owner would be a friend of the sheriff's wife. I looked and saw someone come out of Todd's house and go to the livery and talk to Jeb. Then Jeb saddled a horse for her and I watched as the woman rode off. I ran and jumped on Red and we were on her trail. I followed her in the dark. I had not been for sure who it was cause she was wearing a hooded cape and had not saddled her own horse so to me it seem by the movement it had to be Todd's wife or I assumed that. She led me to near Tom's house. I saw Betty come out on the front porch and the women went down a ways from her horse and Betty went over out of the light to her and they were arguing and Betty shoved the other woman down on the ground. I saw Shelly come out on the porch and look around. I heard her say.

"Mother, is that you out there? Are you talking to someone?"

Todd's wife ran back in the woods then I could hear Betty say.

"No dear I just was taking a little walk. Let's go back inside."

I left behind Todd's wife and she went back to the livery. Coming out of the livery she took off the cape and now I could see it was Todd's wife as she went back into their house. I rode out of town and was confused more than ever. What this had to do with the case I had no idea?

As we ate breakfast the next morning I asked Bonnie.

"Bonnie, what is Todd's wife name?"

"Why it's Maggie. Why do you ask?"

"Just I had a puzzling experience last night. This case has taken an odd turn. Maybe you can help me in this one thing."

"Well I'll be my wife helping a Texas Ranger." Gary said.

"I'll talked to you after breakfast."

"A secret." Gray said again.

After breakfast I told her the whole odd story. She started laughing.

"Jim, since Gary and Tom are becoming friends now Betty and I have been planning a surprise birthday party for Shelly and most of the women are involved and we can't decide whether to have it in town or at the ranch. I bet that is what it's about. I'll go over and talk to Betty and find out what happened last night. I'm glad you didn't spoil it."

"I'll be I had a bad feeling that all the women were involved in the murder case. This eases my mind."

I thought why would Lola be talking to Maggie about me following her to Mexico. There had to be something to that part of it. Maybe it wasn't Maggie what if it was someone else I saw. I didn't know what Maggie looked like."

"Bonnie what does Maggie look like?"

"Let us say that she is a little plump and very short maybe five foot no more."

"Then that wasn't her. This woman was kind of tall for a woman taller than Betty and slim with blond hair in a bun."

"Why that sounds like Sid's wife Mary. I didn't know that she was taking part in planning the party. You know because of Sid's murder. I'll find out the women in town might have got her involved and she went out to find out some things from Betty."

I headed out on the range with the men and it did feel good to get my mind off the case for a while. Sometimes that's when new idea's pop up in my head. That afternoon when we went in for dinner Sara was out in front of the barn waving her arms at us. We all rode over and she said.

"Pa, all of you come in the barn."

We went in and Sara led us to one of the stalls and there was Sleeper with four little pups.

"Look at that, looks like we're going to have some good sheepdogs."

"Pa, can I name them."

"Do y'all mind that?"

"No, just name them a sheepdog name."

Sara said, "Now Pickin's what would that be."

Everyone laughed as we were walking to the house to dinner.

After we ate Bonnie took me to the side.

"Betty said this morning that Mary was helping with the party. She told me that Mary came out last night to talk to her about the party. She said they were discussing it and she patted Mary on the back because she started to cry about how Sid always loved surprise parties. That was when Mary slipped on a rock and fell down. That's when Shelly came out and Mary rushed off."

"That must be all there was to it."

"I think so. I'm glad you didn't spoil the surprise."

All afternoon my mind kept going back and I tried to reason why Lola would be telling Todd and Mary, Sid's wife, about me following her. There had to be a connection somehow. That evening I went to town with Dean and we went straight to the telegraph office.

"You know it's going to be a little harder now that everyone knows who and what I'm doing here."

I sent a telegram to Captain Turbrough telling him I was fine and I would like him to find out about a Mary Whasworth, married to Sid Whasworth a banker. Where she is from and her back ground. Then I went to Red and told Dean.

"Come on around the corner. We're going to see if that man goes anywhere with my telegram or the answer."

"What for?"

"See who is paying to know what I'm doing."

It wasn't five minutes till Gerald come out and went to John's office. He left and John went to the Long Bar. There wasn't enough time for an answer to come back so I let a little information get out.

"Dean, I'll stay here and you mosey over to the Long Bar and see who John went to see."

I saw him walk in and then five minutes later John came out and went to his office. I kept watching both places and Lola came out and went to the bank where Mary had taken over for Sid. She owned it now. Dean came out of the Long Bar and I got his attention and pointed to the bank. He shook his head and went over to the bank and went in. Lola was in there a good while. He came rushing out of the bank and over to me out of breathe. I watched as Lola and Mary came out onto the front walk. Lola put something in her purse and said bye to Mary and hurried back to the Long Bar. Dean got his breath and started talking.

"Lola went to the back office which has a window. I could see them talking and Lola pulled a piece of paper out of her purse and Mary read it then they started arguing. They calmed down then they went outside. I tried to get close enough to make out what was being said but I couldn't."

"That's alright. We'll wait till Gerald come out with the answer. That's when I'll stop him. I'll threaten to get him fired if he tells what came in the reply and let him know that I saw him give Lola my telegram. That may stop him."

"What you doing putting out some more little barbs for them to chew on?"

"Something, like that. They're bound to slip up one day. We'll keep our eyes open cause after this they might think I know too much and try to knock us both off."

We moved to another ally that let us see in every direction. It was getting time for the telegraph office to close so I started to go over there and Gerald came out and saw me and turned and went back inside. We went in.

"Going somewhere Gerald."

"To find you, here's your reply."

"I saw what you did with the telegram I sent. If you tell anyone about this I'll get you fired and believe me I can and you might be in jail."

"No sir, I won't."

"And if they ask? You haven't got a reply back yet."

"That's right."

We left and I had the answer in my hand. I opened it and read the message.

Mary Whasworth was Mary Forman before marrying Sid Whasworth. Both arrested in San Antonio for fraud but let loose for lack of evident five years ago. Before married she was arrested for attempted murder but never proven in Lubbock ten years ago. Not wanted in state of Texas. Jim, be careful those two are dangerous. Last seen in El Paso but be anywhere in west Texas.

Captain Turbrough

"Dean, looks like Mary Whasworth in deep in this but we have to prove it."

"You think she's the only one involved?"

"No, we can't do much right now so let's get out to the ranch."

When we got to the ranch we found out that the surprise birthday party was on Saturday and they wanted me to take Shelly at eight o'clock.

"Bonnie, why me let Dean."

"She likes you and been talking to her mother about you all week. You have to go over there and ask her to go for a buggy ride so she can dress up on her birthday. Keep her away from the big old barn at the end of the street until 8 o'clock. She will be twenty-one."

"I thought it was going to be at Tom's?"

"It was but Mary talked us into having it in town because most people live in town. Now you go get gussied up and go ask that girl tonight."

I went to the bunkhouse and changed into my Sunday go to meeting clothes and rode Red over to Shelly's. I was thinking all the way there. This is not my thing I rather take on two bad men at once than ask a girl out riding and then to a party and dance. I finally got there and Red kind of pushed me on the porch with his head. His wound was healed now and he was a real nuisance. I knocked on the door and there she was all pretty and sweet.

"I heard it was your birthday Saturday and I thought you might want to go for a buggy ride with me."

Her mother poked her head out the door.

"She'd love to."

"Mother, I know what to say. I would love to take a ride with you."

"How about 6:30 it won't be so hot?"

"That will be fine Jim, I'll be ready."

She walked over to Red and looked where the wound was and petted him.

"Look like he's all well."

"Sure is but I was worried at first. We've been together since he was a colt. By the way, why have I not seen you around until the other day? I'll see you Saturday."

"I've been in Dallas visiting a cousin for a while, just got back and first thing I get shot at but I can understand how you felt now about Red. Bye, now. I'll be ready tomorrow."

"Tomorrow, that's right, it is tomorrow. Thank you Shelly."

Dean was still up when I got back to the ranch. I sat down on my bunk and looked at him.

"You know Dean, I asked Shelly to go on a buggy ride tomorrow and then take her to her surprise party. She said yes."

"So, she said yes. Everyone but you could see that she likes you."

"Not that, it gave me an idea. Why don't you go to Marfa and ask June to come to the party with you? We'll have a surprise for a few people especially one murderer."

"I like seeing June but you think it's wise to exposed her to that danger."

"I think we can protect her and with three murders now I have to put an end to this."

"Three murders, I thought only two."

"No, June's grandfather Guy, Sid and now I know Joe was murdered cause of what he was going to tell me."

"I'll leave right now. We don't want June to be next."

"You bring her here to get cleaned up and put on that pretty little dress she wore the night you two met. I'm sure that Bonnie will treat her like family. Tell her it is important to the case and that we'll take care of her and you'll take her back with me behind to see who follows."

Dean packed some grub and saddled his horse and left into the night. It was a ways there and back but I think they could make it in time for the party. I got to bed so late that the morning came fast. At breakfast the women were talking about the party. The men were wondering how many unmarried women would be there. Then Bonnie said.

"Jim, Gary said you can used the buggy this evening and we'll take the wagon into town."

"I don't know about all this."

"You just ride around for an hour and then bring her to the barn and then dance all night."

"Dance! I can't dance." I said and then Sara chimed in with.

"Don't worry after breakfast we'll go to the barn and I'll show you."

"Yea, but!"

"No buts you'll get the hang of it. It's easy."

"Jim, where's Dean this morning." Gary said.

"He went over west of here to ask his girl to the dance. He left late last night. Bonnie I hope you don't mind, I told Dean you probably would let her clean up and change here."

"That will be fine. I didn't know Dean had a girl. What's her name?"

"June and she has to do with my case. They met and I think they really fell for each other."

"Come on Jim to the barn I have to teach you how to dance."

Sara tried, all morning and into the afternoon, to teach me how to dance. I learned some and some was beyond my reach.

"I think you can dance enough to get by just don't try to get fancy."

"Don't worry about that. I better get cleaned up and get the buggy ready."

"I better get it's late. I want to look my best. Some of those cute boys from school might be there. Good luck Jim. See you at the dance."

"Thanks' Sara."

About 5:30 Dean and June came riding in. Them and their horses were covered with dirt and the horses were all lathered up from the hard ride. Gary and me went over with Pickin's behind us. Gary said.

"Pickin's take their horses and cool them down and brush them out get Bob and Slim to help. Now hurry we have a party to go to."

"Y'all two are a sight. Dean, you get to the bunkhouse and get cleaned up. I'll take June to Bonnie and Sara in the house."

Bonnie met June and me at the door and took June.

"Sara and me will take care of this young lady. Jim, you get to Tom's and get Shelly. Now hurry."

"Yes ma'am."

I was off the porch and in the barn in two minutes. The horses were rearing to go and I was all done up. I just hoped I could keep my mind on the case with all the other goings on there was. I hoped I hadn't put June too far out on a limb. I really didn't think that the murderer would want to kill her cause she was the only one that knew where the gold mine was but you never know about the criminal mind. This was a chance and I hoped it paid off. Then I was off down the road to pick up a lovely woman and get her to her surprise party. I was really, really nervous, no one knew it but this is the first time I have taken a girl out anywhere. I kept telling myself it was in the line of duty but my mind knew better. I really liked this woman even with the rocky start we had.

9

I rode up in the front of the house and had the flowers in my hand that Sara and Bonnie had picked for me. I wiped off my boots on the back of my pants and went up the steps and knocked on the front door. The door opened and Tom was staring me in the face.

"Come on in Jim, Shelly will be down in a minute. When you two leave Betty and me will have to hurry to get to town in time. Get her there by eight. Shhh, here they come."

Shelly with her mother behind her looking so proud and Tom had a big smile on his face then I turned and the most beautiful women I had ever seen was coming down the stairs. I went over and took her hand as she stepped off the last step and then I helped her mother off the last step.

"You look mighty beautiful this evening and here are some flowers for a lovely lady and may I say happy birthday."

"Thank you they are so beautiful and you look so handsome. Mother would you put these in some water."

"Yes, honey I will now you two better be off." Then Tom spoke.

"I would say to be careful and mind your manners but you be a Texas Ranger I don't think that's necessary."

"Now, Dad! I know I'll be fine."

"You better be off." Betty said.

As we left we heard all this commotion from inside the house. I knew they were rushing to get ready. Then Shelly said.

"I wonder what's going on with those two."

I helped her in the buggy and she got her dress straighten out. As I got in I told her.

"That dress looks so beautiful on you."

"Thank you, now where are you taking me."

"Well, I know you've probably seen most of the places around here but I found a nice spot the other day I thought I'd show you and we can sit and talk awhile and then I want to take you to the diner in town."

"That sound's lovely. Now where's this spot."

"We'll be there in no time."

I headed east so we could come in town on the side that her party was at. We rode up two or three small rises.

"You know, you may be wrong I don't think that I've ever been over this way and this road hasn't been used much."

"I was just looking for tracks one day and came across this. Wait till you see it, the sight will take your breath away."

"Hurry, I can't wait."

"It's over the next rise."

The road made a sharp curve to the right and then a sharp curve to the left and there was a shear drop off to the left and down the center was a deep crevice and to the right there was shear rock that went up over a hundred feet and we were climbing up a steep incline when we reached the top the horses were sure winded by the climb. As we stopped I saw the look in Shelly's eyes and I knew that she had not ever seen this sight but she loved the beauty as much as I did.

"Jim, I never could have imagine that this place would be this close to our ranch. I bet Dad's never seen this."

"With that road or more like a trail not many people may know about this."

As we got down to let the horses rest we looked out over a lush green valley that didn't match anything around this part of the country. There were trees tall as a three story building in Dallas.

"There has to be some kind of water source down there. Look over there where the trees are lining each side of something and how it curves like a river but the trees are so large you can't tell from here." Shelly said.

"Look to the right, that may be a small waterfall. One day when this case is over I was thinking that we could find a way in there on horseback if you would like to. You know I won't be a Ranger all my life and this would be a good spot to settle down if there is a good place for a house and I'm sure there's plenty of grass."

"I would love to do that. I love to horseback ride and explore. Look over to that thick stand of trees over by that waterfall. Is that a roof of a small cabin?"

"I can't tell from here but we'll find out soon. Right now we better had get back to town before it gets dark. This is a bad road in the daylight much less dark."

We went back down and I turned on another trail that I knew came out right east of town. That's when Shelly said.

"You mention your case. I'm been thinking about that day I saw that older man follow June and John was there."

"Yes, have you remembered something else?"

"There was also a woman she was about middle age, and she looked about two inches shorter than John and she was dressed nice and had a cape on with a hood that covered her head. I couldn't see what she looked like because of the hood. When John went to his office she went to a house down near the bank."

"The older man, did you remember anything about him?"

"I know I have never seen him before or since but he was about an inch taller than John and I could see grey hair coming out from under his hat. Oh, he had a mustache that turned up on the ends."

"You think you might recognize him if you saw him."

"I'm pretty sure I would."

"Let me know if you think of anything else and we may get to explore that valley soon and find out if anyone lives in that cabin."

We both laughed out loud.

"That would be nice."

We were now close to town and I had to think of some reason to stop at the large barn outside of town. As I turned the horses around the next corner there was a bunch of buggies, wagons and horses around the old barn. She said.

"I wonder what in the world is going on here. This barn has been deserted for years."

"Maybe there's something going on that no one told us about. Let's go in and see what it maybe."

"I don't know we might be intruding on something important."

"You said you like to explore let us go exploring."

'Alright we'll do it."

I tied up the horses and I took her hand as she stepped down from the buggy and we walked to the door of the barn. There was no sound coming out from the barn and as I opened the barn door a crack it was dark inside. Shelly said out loud.

"My goodness, what is going on in here?" As she looked around into the dark inside the barn.

I threw the doors wide open and the lights started to come on as the lanterns were being lit and at the same time the voices of everyone inside yelled.

"Surprise, happy birthday!"

Shelly threw her hands in the air and looked at me.

"You! You knew about this."

"Yes, I did."

I left my gun and hat by the door where all the other men had. Then most everyone gathered around and wished her a happy birthday. As I looked over in one corner there were Mary, Lola, Chance and Ted all talking and looking over the other way. As I looked there beside Dean was June and she had the four's attention. Dean took June up to meet Shelly and then as they got closer to us Shelly recognized June and rushed toward her and hugged June.

"June, it's been a long time and with Dean well what a small world. You got a good one there."

"Hello Shelly, I think he is. You know I remember when we use to play in front of the general store. That was so long ago."

"I saw you here in Alpine a few months ago but you must had been in a hurry."

As the band started to play we went over to the side and they continued to talk as the guest started dancing.

"How are you Jim, any word yet?"

"Some new developments, but Shelly I didn't know that June was the girl that you played with that you told me about."

"I didn't know you knew each other. Anyway it was a long while ago." Shelly said.

Dean asked June to dance and they took the dance floor and Shelly looked at me and Sara was beside me and nudged me in the side.

"Jim, ask her to dance she's your date."

"I don't know if I can do this in front of all these people."

Shelly said, "What are you two talking about?"

"Well, Shelly I'm nervous, I want to dance with you but Sara just showed me a little this afternoon and I don't know if I can."

"Come on I'll take it easy on you big fella. I just want to be in your arms dancing."

Shelly pulled me and Sara pushed me and they got me on the dance floor and then it came back to me and we were dancing around the dance floor and I looked over and Sara was smiling. Then a boy asked her to dance. It wasn't so bad and Shelly felt so good in my arms that the case nearly went out of my head as we went around and around. The music stopped and Shelly, June, Dean and me went to the punch bowl and then I looked over and kept an eye on the four suspects and then the music played again.

"Would you excuse me Shelly I would like to dance with my teacher once?"

"Go ahead Jim how sweet of you."

As I took Sara to the dance floor I saw Gary ask Shelly to dance and Tom ask Bonnie to dance. Then I noticed Dean was keeping a close watch on June as they went around the dance floor. Then a young man tapped me on the shoulder and I gave Sara's hand to him and they went away dancing and Sara had a big smile on her face. I got some punch as the music played on and went over to where the four were. That's when I saw John dancing with his wife.

"Why, hello Chance I didn't know that you knew Mary so well. You haven't left her side all night."

"I just met her tonight and we seemed to get along." Chance said.

Then Mary interrupted us. "I don't think it's any of your business. Why don't you go watch Dean's little girl friend and give Dean a break? He won't let her out of his sight."

"Now isn't that too bad. Lola good to see you I think you should have never come back from Mexico."

The music stopped and I went over to where Shelly, Dean and June was.

"This is turning out to be a great night. We have found old friends and met some new ones and now Shelly may I have this dance."

"Yes, you may sir."

As we were dancing I saw that Ted had left the little group and went out of the barn and then Shelly asked.

"I didn't know you knew Mary Whasworth?"

"I really don't, just met her a while ago over there. But I've seen her before riding her horse at night. All four of those are involved in my case somehow but tonight is yours, my birthday girl so get that out of your mind and just let me hold you and dance the night away."

"That I will do."

The night went by and people were eating and dancing and then Shelly blow out the candles on her birthday cake and she cut the cake and I passed out the plates of cake as Shelly's friends came up. We sang happy birthday to her and then it was time for Shelly to open her presents. As she opened each present people would o-o-o and ah, ah about how pretty and nice everything was. Then as people were starting to leave a gun shot went off from behind the barn. "Dean, stay here and watch out for June and Shelly. I'll be back as soon as I can."

I ran for the door and picked out my gun and hat and looked around to find Mary, Lola and Chance and they were gone and John was already out of the barn and we ran down the side to the back of the barn and as I turned the corner there were people all around the body. When I got closer I could see a lone rider leave out of town to the east. As I turned and made my way through the crowd I looked down and there was Ted on the ground.

John said, "Jim, he was shot in the back. He's dead."

"John, I saw a lone rider leaving to the east."

John had his horse then he was away and I borrowed Pickin's horse and I was right behind him. This is one time that Red would be back in the barn. I just barely kept up with John and then he yelled back.

"I can see a shadow up ahead."

As we drew closer the shadow disappeared off the road. When we got to the spot where the rider left the road we stopped.

"Where did he go?" I said.

"He left the road right here, but I don't see any kind of trail. The brush is so thick and it's so dark. Let's go back I'll come out here in the morning when it's daylight."

"I guess you're right, we would just cut up the horses through that brush in the dark."

We headed back, most everyone was gone when we got to the barn but there out in front was Shelly, June and Dean with Pickin's along with Tom and Betty.

"He got away, thanks Pickin's."

I went over to Shelly.

"Sorry that this happened at your party. Bonnie came over.

"June, you spend the night in Sara's room Dean can take you home in the morning. It's too dangerous on the trail at night."

"Thank You."

"Tom, we'll follow you home. With that killer out there it will be safer."

"I was waiting for you just for that reason."

I helped Shelly in the buggy and we took the lead back to the ranch. Gary was driving their wagon with Bonnie by his side and Dean and June with Sara in the back. When we got to the Y Gary went left and we went right. We rode up and Tom and Betty went inside and we talked for a while.

"I'm really sorry we had all the goings on at the end there."

"I really had a great time until then." She smiled and then continued. "See you can dance fine."

"I guess so, you were right just get out there and have some fun."

"That's all there is to it. I'm looking forward to that ride down in that valley."

"That is pretty and we'll see it together one day. I may have to go down that way tomorrow that killer went down in the brush that way. I'll find a way down for us to go later."

"Good night, I better get in now."

I took off my hat and put my arm around her waist and drew her to me and kissed her on the lips as she came toward me.

"For one thing, I didn't have to teach you how to kiss. Good night."

I felt myself turn red when she said that and said.

"Good night, I'll see you soon."

As she went in the door she said. "You be careful you hear me."

"Yes ma'am."

All the way back to the ranch I was thinking about that valley and how that man disappeared off the road and no sign of him leaving it.

The next morning I left for town early. By the time I got to John's office he had his horse ready and we were down the east road out of town. We came to where we both thought the rider left the road. I got down off Red and looked for tracks leading into the brush. We walked our horses for a mile and no luck. John looked at me.

"I was sure it was around here but not a sign of a track."

"You think they could have come back later and brushed them out."

"Could be, it's their life we're trying to take."

"John, I'm glad we're alone. Want to talk to you. I have been watching Mary, Chance and Lola and I was watching Ted. When I sent the Captain that telegram I saw Gerald talk to you and then you showed it to Chance and Lola. I don't want to think that you are involved in all this but I hope you can explain why you did that. Cause we're talking about four murders now. Cause I don't want you to have to trade your pretty little wife for a gallows."

"Jim, I'm going to tell you the truth. This town doesn't pay me very much and I don't like to deprive Paula of anything she wants and that's not much. So I do little favors for the people that run the town. Lola is one of them. I gave her that telegram and she gave me twenty dollars. I do the same for Jeb and Todd and for Sid when he was alive. If any of them are involved with murder I know nothing about it. I hope you believe me."

"I've know you a long time so I don't think you had anything to do with murder but don't do anything for them anymore, at least till this case is over. This looks like a dead end why don't you go back to town and I'm going to look around awhile longer. And John if you see any of those upstanding citizen doing anything out of the ordinary let me know and right now I'm still your friend."

"That's a deal."

John went back to town and I kept looking up and down the road. Red was wondering if I ever would ride him again. I was sticking my hand in the brush and pulling on it to see if any brush would come loose. It was a hot and lousy time of year for this. It happened six miles out of town on the road that started to curve and go up. A large juniper bush came right out of the ground. Then I saw it hadn't been in the ground at all. It had been wedged in between two other bushes. Then I cleared a path about ten feet from the road. I now saw a path going down toward the valley. The brush around the trail was tall enough to block the view of the trail from the road. As I went further down it widen out to a good ten feet wide. It was wide enough to mount Red and head down. The trail was steep in places but Red had run the trails in Colorado and I knew him to be sure footed. It was a plain trail that had been used so frequently that it kept the brush down. I was taking it easy going down cause I didn't know what to expect. It took us an hour to reach the bottom and as I had expected the floor of the valley was something to lay your eyes on. As I moved to the northwest the brush turn to tall, lush trees and the dirt turn to green grass. We rode upon! Why right in front of me there was a steam that flowed from the north to the south. I got down and let Red drink and graze on some green grass and I took my hat off and dipped it in the water and drank and put my wet hat back on my head it felt so good. Then I soaked my bandana in the water and wrapped it back around my neck. It was so good and cold. I just couldn't believe it. My attention was averted just a second to long, as I saw the sun reflect off some metal object and then I heard a shot but too late as it hit me.

When I woke up it was dark and I had a pounding in my head. Red was still standing in the patch of grass. It was hard to move and when I put my hand to my head I could barely see the blood in my hand. I took off my bandana again and dipped it back in the stream and rubbed my head. When I got all the blood off I could feel a deep crease on the back of my head. I was sort of dizzy and had to pull myself up by the stirrup. I managed to get in the saddle.

"Red, take it slow going up."

I would have to find out what was down here another day. I'm just glad that whoever did this didn't come check on their work or I would be dead. Red worked his way up the trail and I just barely stayed in the saddle. Once on the road I put the brush back like it was. It took me an hour and I then took the cut off around town and headed to the ranch. Red took his time and I passed out two or three times. I felt the back of my head and the blood was starting to flow again. It was late cause the half-moon was half ways across the sky. I came into the ranch yard and the dogs started barking then Red started whinnying and I saw lanterns coming on in the house and bunkhouse and there were figures and then I fell off Red and hit the ground hard. Bonnie was the first one to me.

"Got shot, not too bad, don't get doc; you take care; don't tell anyone in town; not John; say I can't be found. Tell Dean to keep eye on things in town. Don't take any chances."

"Alright, Jim, boys get him in the house in Sara's bed."

That's when the lights went out. I woke up and Sara was sitting by me.

"Hello Sara, how are you?"

"I should be asking you that. Ma, he's awake and sassy."

Bonnie came in the room wiping her hands on a towel and looked at me.

"'Bout time you woke up. Now I can get some broth in you."

"How long have I been out?"

"Two days this morning."

"Red alright? If it wasn't for him I would be dead and still in that canyon. Is Dean here?"

"Yea, came in yesterday from taking June home. Sara, go get Dean, tell him Jim's awake."

"How's my head? It feels like it's going to fall off."

"I should have not listen to you and got the doc. I think you have a concussion. But I don't know. I know doc keeps his patients in bed with a concussion. So that's where you been and that's where you'll stay for two more days."

She left the room and came back with some broth and made me drink all of it.

"Tomorrow you can get some whole food if you can keep it down. It's plain to see what happened to you but where did it happen."

"Down in the prettiest little valley. That's why I got shot cause I was admiring the sights and not paying attention."

About then Dean came in and Bonnie left.

"You sure lookin' a little better."

"I still feel like I got ran over by a team of horses and the wagon went over me to. How'd it go taking June back, any trouble."

"I shouldn't tell you; you would try to get on Red and leave."
"What happened Dean?"

"That's where it's a little touchy. I didn't know what to make of it."

"What Dean?"

"We were riding, about half way to Marfa, when we saw a buggy coming toward us. It was Todd and his wife Maggie. They said they were in Marfa looking at the old store. They hoped one day the town would come alive again. Said they still owned the building that the general store is in. They wondered how the store stayed so clean. June didn't say a word. Funny thing is they would have to had left right after the dance to meet us coming back. When we got there we had to hide the horses and she took me to one of her hiding places, she said that she has many, cause there was a tall stranger in the town. I've never seen him. June said he looked familiar from way back, but she didn't know."

"Any talk in town about where I am or what happened to me?"

"John asked but I told him that nobody has seen you. He told me that he left you on the road east of town looking for tracks."

"I said I would look down that way. Then Lola and Chance asked but I just told them that they better be careful if they didn't want to end up like their friend Ted. They just looked at each other puzzled."

"Dean, you shouldn't have taken a risk like that. We don't know if one of them killed those people."

"It looks like we're getting rid of most bad people, except June's grandfather that was good as I see it."

"One of them thinks that the last one alive will get the gold mine."

"Keep your eyes open cause I'm going to be laid up two more days."

"I'll let you get some rest."

I fell asleep and when I woke up Sara was again sitting by me.

"Hello, this is your bed. Where you sleeping?"

"In the front room. Mother made a pallet for me at night and I pick it up in the morning."

"I'm sorry, I took your bed."

"That's alright, reminds me of when I was little and snuck in there and slept on the divan."

"How's Gary coming along with getting ready for the sheep shearing?"

"Good, Dean and you did most of the work in the shearing barn and ma is sharping the shears. The men are moving the sheep down from the mountains and valleys into pastures closer to the barn. Pa made arrangements with the railroad to ship the wool to Chicago. That's where buyers come from all over the country to buy wool."

"Does your pa store the wool in the barn till the wool is to be loaded on the train?"

"No, we don't have enough space. We store it in that big old barn that we had the party in."

"Sara, when your pa comes in from the range would ask him to come see me."

"I will. You must have an idea because the color just came back to your face."

"Yes I did. I need to get out of the bed soon as I can."

10

I went to sleep and didn't wake up for three or four hours and Sara was there with my broth and I drank it down as fast as I could. Then after supper Gary came in to see me.

"Heard you wanted to talk to me? You sure look better than you did two nights ago."

"I been laying here thinking. They tried to steal your sheep and we caught two men. What if they or Bart weren't the one's behind the stealing. I think Joe was going to tell me who was behind it all and that's why he was killed. They may still want your ranch. Sara and I was talking about the sheep shearing coming up and she said that you stored the wool in that old barn east of town till the train brings cars to take it to Chicago."

"As we shear the sheep we load the wool in the wagons and take it to that old barn. What are you getting at Jim? You must be feeling better to be thinking this much."

"I'm getting at, whoever is behind this and the murders may try to burn that old barn with all that wool in it."

"That would sure ruin me. What can be done?"

"We're going to have to guard that barn around the clock till that train arrives. Or maybe I can rap this case up before then. Tomorrow morning Dean and me are heading down to where I was shot. That place is near impossible to reach. I think maybe the brains behind all the trouble and murders may be down there."

"You sure you should get out. You're still weak."

"I have to, someone thinks they killed me so I need to react now while they are unaware."

In the morning, after spending the night in the bunkhouse against Bonnie's wish, Dean and me rode out and it felt good to be out on Red again with the wind in my face and the open sky above me. We rode up the street of Alpine and stopped in front of the sheriff's office. John came out and looked straight at me with amazement in his eyes.

"What's a matter John think you're looking at a ghost? Well, you're not, just been laid up for a while."

"No, just we hadn't seen you and everyone thought you might had left town."

"I told you before I hoped that you weren't involved so I'm just letting you know to stay out of my way. I'm going to bust this thing wide open. If I'm killed there will be a whole company of Rangers on the way here. Someone knew that I was out near that trail when I was shot and as far as I know you were the only one."

"I didn't know you were shot. If you need any help I'll be here."

We left and I went to the saloon. Chance and Lola were sitting at a table as we walked in.

"Where you been? We're not open yet." Chance said.

"I know I just wanted you two to see me, see that I was still around."

"We don't care one way or another." Lola said.

We headed out of town but slowed down in front of Mary Whasworth house and she was there at the window looking straight at me. I tipped my hat and we rode on but not out of town. We stopped around the corner where the livery was.

"Dean, we'll just sit here awhile and see what develops now that they know I wasn't killed."

"You sure let them have it especially John. You really think he's in on the murders."

"I sure hope not. But when you told him that you hadn't seen me he didn't go lookin' for me and he knew where he had left me and what I was looking for. Well, look there, Dean."

We were watching as Lola and Maggie came out on the street and went straight to Mary's house. They were looking both ways and met in the middle of the street and went on to Mary's and the door opened just as they went up the steps. Then we heard a horse leave from in back of the general store and as we looked we saw Todd leaving town to the east right behind where we were.

"You sure stirred up a hornets nest."

"Just what I intended to do. Why lookey there."

There was Chance heading west out of town. So far not a move from John and that was good as far as I was concerned. I had no idea where Chance was going but I knew a trail down to the valley and that is the direction Todd was going so we followed Todd. We kept a ways behind Todd so he wouldn't see us but when we reached the trail that I had found that led to the floor of the valley he had kept on going.

"Dean, we're going down here. Down there is where I got shot."

"Where, I don't see a trail."

I pulled back the brush and there was the trail and we went down and as we reached the bottom I showed Dean the place that I had been shot.

"When Shelly and me were looking down in this valley from up above we thought that there was some kind of a building somewhere down here. It must be to the north."

"I never knew something like this existed anywhere around here."

"Keep your eyes open, that's how I got shot looking at this wonder."

Across the stream we headed north the way I had been going the day I was shot. The brush was now a thing of the past and before us lay lush, green valley and there were two more streams to cross. At the second stream I headed east the way the stream was going. It was amazing cause all around us were large pine trees and when we had followed the stream for two miles the stream disappeared into a wall of rock. We turned northwest and kept in line with a mountain that I had spotted early.

"When this is over I'm going to bring Shelly down here and explore where that stream comes out on the other side of that wall of rock."

"You know it could head underground that's why the rest of the country is so dry around here."

We kept heading the same direction and then we spotted them.

"Look, some of Tom's cattle grazing on that grass look at the brand. They knew this valley was so well hidden that the brand wasn't even tampered with. This must be where most of his cattle were going. We may run into some sheep around here."

"There's bound to be a cabin around here somewhere and you noticed that we hadn't passed any fences."

"The water and grass keeps them here and then the natural boundaries. There has to be another way in this place cause these cattle couldn't come down that small trail that we came down without being noticed by someone over the years."

We turned around the next bend of rocks and we saw smoke coming up through the trees.

"Dean, look over there above the trees, smoke. We'll leave the horses here and go on foot."

The trees were thick here and there was no problem with being seen as long as we were careful. When we reached a little cleaning we could see across a small pasture the back of a large cabin. We made our way around the cleaning staying among the trees. When we were within a hundred yards we stopped and I got out my spyglass and could see the front of the cabin clearly. There came a clapper of horse hoofs and two men came into view. It was Chance and Todd coming in from to different directions.

"Look Dean."

He took the glass and looked and then said.

"There's a third man that came out of the house."

"You recognize him?"

"No, never seen him in town."

"Let me look."

I took the spyglass and got a good look. A man in his early fifties with gray hair that was long for a man and a mustache that was gray. He didn't have on range clothes but a suit that belonged in a large city that a lawyer would wear. I watched for a while and out of the cabin came a young woman about twenty-five years old and she was way along pregnant. The older man shooed her back in the cabin.

"Are we going to rush them?"

"No Dean, I think I've seen enough let's get back to the horses and head to town the same way we came in."

"We have stolen cattle that's enough to hang them."

"We need to get the whole bunch for murder. We know where to find the leader or one of the leaders if we need him. Not a word of this to anyone not even June that might put her in more danger. Now let's go."

We got back to our horses and made it back to the trail going up to the main road. I replaced the brush. When we got to town I went straight to John's office.

"Dean you want to head back to the ranch or come in. I remember a picture in John's office I need to look at."

"I'll get to the ranch; Gary will need help driving the sheep in from the high pastures. You know the shearing is in a week. I'll see you later."

"Remember not a word about what we found."

"Sure, Jim."

I went into the sheriff's office and walked over to the wall by the cells. There was a picture and I was staring at it when John walked up.

"Can I help you with something Jim."

"When was this picture taken?"

"I'd say about twenty years ago. That's me on the left."

"I'd say you were a handsome fellow in those days."

"My wife still says that I am but I think she just remembers the good old days."

"Who is the other fellow in the picture?"

"That's Jimmy Johnson we were real close back then."

"Can you tell me more about him?"

"Sure, I was the sheriff here in Alpine and he was the marshal in Marfa. We helped each other when we had trouble sometimes. His wife and Paula were close. When Marfa was deserted he took off for other places. I heard later his wife died and he was broke up about it. I did see him one more time about five years ago right here in Alpine. Down the street he was talking to Mary Whasworth. I came up and Mary left for home. He said he was investigating a missing girl for a client. He pointed her out. She looked to be dressed in men's clothes but I could tell she looked to be seventeen or so. When she left town he was right behind her. That's the last time I saw him."

"Do you know of any pregnant young women around here maybe twenty-four or five that may have disappeared a few month ago?"

John scratched his chin and looked at me like he was staring right through me.

"Are you just curious or does it have to do with your case or these murders."

"I think it could be linked with the murders and the murder that brought me here."

"Not to many people around here know this but about seven months ago there was another girl that worked in the Long Bar for Lola. Her name was Stella and it was rumored that she took men up to her room sometimes. Well, Sid Whasworth was one of those men. To make a long story short Mary found out about Stella and Sid and it was said that Stella was going to have a baby, Sid's baby. It was bad enough about Sid and Stella but when Mary found out about the baby she threatened to kill Sid. Everyone knew she couldn't ever have a baby but I think she just ran Stella out of town cause she disappeared and hasn't been seen again."

"That may be the connection with the murders. I'm sorry about being so hard on you this morning. I thought you might be involved but now I'm sure you're not."

"That I'm glad of I told that group of people no more little favors. I can't get in trouble this late in life. A couple of years and I'll retire. Maybe buy a little ranch."

As I left town I turned to look back, a habit that I couldn't break, there was John leaving his office and went right to Mary's house and went inside as she opened the door. I thought about this all the way back to the ranch. The sun was heading below the horizon as I rode up to the house. It looked to me that I was going to take a couple of days off from the case to help Gary with the sheep shearing. This case was getting more intense and more complicated by the day. It was no longer just the killing of Guy Grayson but of three other people. Right now I didn't know for sure if the cases were linked together. I have a feeling it is all about the gold. I was quiet at supper my mind was taken up by this case. I did manage to let Gary know that I would be there to help with the sheep and help protect the barn till the train was away with all the wool. I had a restless night and the next morning Dean came in and got me up.

"Come on outside and see who just rode in with his wife and two children."

I got into my pants, shirt, and boots then I put my hat and gun belt on and headed out. There in front of the house, big as life, was Big Tim. All the men and Gary and his family were standing there looking at this big man with his family.

"Me come bring family want to work with sheep. Tired of tracking for bad people. Want to be with family."

"Gary, this is Big Tim, Dean and me met him down in Mexico. He said he knew everything about sheep and I knew with Joe about to be sent to prison you would need some help. So I invited him to come here."

"I do need help and if he knows about sheep. Well, Big Tim I'll let you work with us for three or four days and if I like the way you work you will have a permanent job. Now we only have a bunkhouse for the men. I don't know about your family. We will be sheering next week."

"That alright we stay in wagon down by stream till get permanent job then we find permanent place to stay. Wife can help with cooking and sheering. We know all about sheering and our children can help with the wool. They do good job."

"You get your family settled and then you can start tomorrow."

"No, start now wife know what to do. She set up camp many time. I ready go now with men."

"That's good, alright let's go to work. Sara, show Big Tim's wife the way to the stream and help her if you can."

"Yes, pa."

"Wife name Little Fawn and this is Chico and this little one is Blue Deer."

The men left and Big Tim was with them.

"Sara, let me help."

"Good, we don't know if they speak English."

Little Fawn spoke. "Me and children speak English. Big Tim made us go to the mission school. Husband say we need to get along with white man so children can have better life."

Sara said. "Follow me Little Fawn, Jim you can come to."

"Thank you Sara."

Bonnie ran in the house and came out with some foodstuff and handed them to Little Fawn.

"These are for your family your husband works for us we provide the food. You can eat with us anytime up at the house. If you need more food come here and I'll let you have it. After you get settled you can work with Sara and me if you want to and Gray will pay you extra. Your children will get along fine playing around here."

"Children can work to. If have a garden they can keep weeds out and keep it watered for you."

"That's fine, good to have you here, Little Fawn."

We led Big Tim's family to a nice spot on a running brook and we helped her set up camp. When we were done I left and Sara stayed to talk to Little Fawn and Chico that was ten and Blue Dear that was seven. I could see that the whole family were hard workers and would be an asset to this ranch. I took a ride over to see Shelly and on the way to the Davis ranch I kept a lookout for a place that could possibly led down into that valley. Most of what I saw was sheer rock. As I reached the ranch looking for a way in left my mind and was replaced by Shelly and the enjoyment we had at the dance and on our ride. Shelly was on the front porch. As she came down the steps I dismounted Red and removed my hat.

"Such a gentleman, now what are you doing here?"

"For one thing I wanted to see you. To look at you for a while."

"Why Jim you make a lady blush."

"We sure had a fine time the other night till the other goings on. That's the other reason I'm out this way. Dean and me found a trail, if it could be called that, down into our valley. I came this way trying to find another way in, one that would be easier and maybe a buggy could get in there. That was after I got shot."

"Shot! She said as her hand went over her mouth.

"It was deeper than when you shot at me. I was out for two days and if it hadn't been for Red I would had died down in that lovely valley."

"Now if you're going a looking, I'm going with you."

"No, Shelly it's too dangerous. I'm looking for murders and may run into them."

"Mr. Jim Beddly, you might as well get used to me right now. I always do what I want."

"Alright, I can't resist you. We probably won't find anyway in there and it will be a good ride and we can get to know each other a little more."

"Let me tell mother that I'm going on a ride. I'm already in my riding pants."

When she came out of the house we went to the barn and I saddled her horse and we were off heading east of the ranch. We rode across grass pastures that were dying cause of the west Texas heat. Then we turned more to the north where we could see some mountains and as we came closer we could see a shear wall of rock that rose up into the sky.

"That doesn't look very promising. That would be impossible to get through or over."

"I don't know let's follow it awhile. There may be a break in the rock face down the way."

We rode as close to the rock face as we could get for all the brush was so grown up that the horses had a hard time so in some places I got down and pulled on the brush to see if it was loose. In some places the vines covered the face up to twenty feet. "Jim, I think this is useless."

"There has to be some way to get by this barrier."

We continued on and came into some thick pine trees.

"You know these pines look like the ones in the valley. Dean and me found three streams on the floor of the valley. One we followed and it went under a formation like this. We couldn't get to the other side but I bet the streams go underground and this is where the stream is under the surface. Why else would these pines be here with no water source near that I can see?"

"Jim, you hear that. Sounds like a buggy."

"Come on let's get back in the brush over here. Red, you be quiet."

I watched through my spyglass; we were about a quarter of a mile away then a buggy rode right up to the wall and stopped.

"Look Shelly, that's Mary."

"I wonder what's she doing out here. Look she's getting down."

She walked to the wall and reached into the brush and pulled out a rope and started pulling down on the rope hand over hand. As Mary pulled on the rope the bottom of the rock face started to rise and as she pulled the rope more the higher the rock and brush would rise till there was an opening. She got in the buggy and went through to the other side and got down and untied the rope and lowered the brush back in place. From where we were it looked just like the brush and rock we had been following for miles.

"Let's go Jim."

"Not yet, let her get down that road we saw."

We waited a good twenty minutes and headed to where Mary went through the rock. We had to search for a good time and finally found the right place and I reached through and untied the rope.

"Shelly, I think you should go back home and wait for me."

"Not on your life, I want to find out what's going on."

"These people may have killed four people. Two more won't matter to them."

"Pull on that rope Jim and let's get going. Anyway I'm with a Texas Ranger."

"If anything happens to you your father will have my hide. I shouldn't do this but here goes. You promise to do what I say."

"I will, Jim."

"If I say get out can you get this up to leave in a hurry."

"If Mary can get this rock up I can."

I started pulling the rope down and the brush and rock started up just like before and there before us was a well-developed road leading as far as we could see. We went through and closed the gate and I led the way into the pine forest that was before us now that we were off the road. Then we saw a creek that was full of water it came from under the rock formation that we had come through. There wasn't a creek on the other side of the wall. We were about two hundred feet from the road in the rough fringes of the woods and the pines were a good hundred feet tall and cause of all the shade under the trees there was not much brush to kept us from being seen. The road curved to the left then to the right then once in a while I would take out my spyglass and look all around but I saw nothing. We kept this up for about three miles and then in front of us was the house that Dean and me had seen. It was sitting back off the road a ways and smoke was coming out of the chimney and there in front was Mary's buggy.

"Let's leave the horses tied up here. Watch for some men, they must have some around here somewhere."

"We don't want to get shot like the last time you were here by yourself."

I led the way toward the house slowly trying not to make any noise and not be seen. I had to give Shelly credit she kept up with me and wasn't making any noise till she tripped on a log laying across our path. That caused her to fall right on her face but the ground was covered with soft pine needles so she got up and dusted herself off and caught up with me. It was then that I caught a movement off to our right then I realized that there were two men moving our way, they must had heard the noise when Shelly fell. They were a good hundred yards so I searched for a place to hide. I grabbed Shelly's hand and moved quickly to where I saw some covering. We ducked behind some boulders then as we stood there waiting for the men to tire and go back to the house I heard a footfall in the leaves behind us and as I started to turn Shelly yelled.

"Jim, watch out."

It was too late and as I looked at Shelly I felt a glancing blew to the side of my head and I felt myself falling. I tried to get up but I was knocked down again with a gun barrel and I was out.

11

When I came to I couldn't move and my head felt like a sledgehammer was inside. I kept still and opened my eyes a little. I could see Shelly tied to a chair to the left of me. My hands were bound behind me and to the chair I was sitting in. My head was starting to clear and I kept quiet cause I didn't want Shelly to know I had regained consciousness till I knew what was going on. I thought we might not have much time to live now that I knew their hideout. There were some footsteps coming so I kept my eyes closed and listened as the door opened. I heard two voices; one was Mary's and the other I didn't recognize but it was a man.

Mary said, "What are we going to do with these two?"

Then Shelly said, "You're going to let us go or my father will hunt you down to the end of the earth and you won't get a trial he'll just kill you."

The man said, "Your father, we stole his cattle for near a year to get capital to operate this place and he wasn't ever close to us until this Ranger came around."

I opened my eyes just a slit so I could see if I recognized this man. I could barely see him but there was no doubt about it. There in front of us was Jimmy Johnson. I closed my eyes again.

"We'll bury them out in the pine woods and they will never find them or this place."

"The girl is right; Tom I know and he adores his daughter and he will never give up. This isn't the same as that old prospector that died before he told us where the gold mine was. He only had a little granddaughter, and they might find them and this place, these two did."

"Yea, but we can't even catch that girl so she will tells us where that gold mine is."

Then I heard a third voice it must be Stella that came in the room.

"What's going to happen now? I'm 'bout to have this kid you and Jimmy wanted so bad. A baby won't do us much good if we have to run. I had to sleep with that dirty old man of yours cause you couldn't have no baby."

Mary was mad and yelling at Stella, "You shut your mouth you little whore or I'll shut it permanent like I did Sid's."

"You won't hurt me till I have this kid. When you're away Jimmy don't mind sleeping with this little pregnant whore. You didn't want me sleeping with Jimmy cause he was your man and now he is."

"You shut your filthy little mouth and for you Jimmy, what do you have to say?"

"She's lying just to get you off her back remember I had to kill Joe cause he saw you with Bart and Shorty and was going to tell this Ranger who you were. So don't get on my back."

Shelly spoke up very calm. "Before y'all kill each other why don't you let us go."

"You shut your mouth or I'll kill you right now." Mary went on.

It was about time I made my presence known. I had heard enough to hang them both and send Stella away for a long time. I started moving and acting like I was just regaining consciousness. I opened my eyes and looked surprised that I was tied up and I could see that my hat was on the floor and there was blood dripping from my head on to my lap. I tried to stretch to loosen the rope.

"You might as well stop struggling that will just make the ropes tighter."

"You alright Shelly?"

"For now I am. But they want to kill us."

"What for? We were just looking around this pretty little valley."

"You shut your mouth or I'll shut it for you again."

"Big man, when my hands are tied. If we aren't back Tom will start looking for us. You let us go and we'll forget about the whole thing."

"You're real funny and I believe in Santa Clause."

The three of them left the room and I started pulling the ropes really tight and then relaxed and the ropes would loosen a mite. They had not taken my spurs off my boots so I had to reach them. My feet hadn't been tied so I could move them freely. I could barely hear them in the other room.

"We have to get rid of them and go to Marfa and look for that girl for as long as it takes."

I whispered, "Shelly, did you tell anyone where we were going."

"I didn't know for sure so I only told Mother that we were going riding but she'll tell dad when we don't come back. I just hope she doesn't wait to long."

*****

"Tom, I'm worried they've been gone an awful long time."

"You know them, they're probably eating supper at Gray's you know she's become close to that family since Gary and me settled our little dispute."

"I know that's true but I just have a feeling that they might be in trouble and with a murderer around and her with Jim they might have come across something."

"Alright Betty, I'll ride over there right now."

Tom headed over to Gary's in hopes that Shelly would be there sitting around the supper table. It worried him a little cause Betty didn't get these feeling very often but when she did she was usually right. As Tom rode up to the ranch house he started to worry even more cause Shelly's horse wasn't out in front. As he got off his horse the front door opened and Gary and Bonnie came out.

"Good to see you Tom." Gary said.

"Come in for supper." Bonnie told him.

"I would but I'm out looking for Shelly and Jim. He came over and took Shelly riding and Betty's worried. That was this morning and with Jim looking for a murderer, I'm a little concern myself."

"Tell you what I'll get Dean he's been working with Jim he might know where he might be at."

Gary took off to the bunkhouse and the men were just coming up for supper.

"Dean, Tom's here and Jim took Shelly riding early this morning and him and Betty are worried. I thought you might know where they might be off to."

"Hello Tom, I know that they had been looking at a valley from a ridge. In fact Jim found a trail down into that valley. That's where he got shot. After that we went back down there and found some of your cattle and a house. That trail was steep and rough and Jim didn't want to say anything till he found a better way in there. Let me get saddled and we'll go get Big Tim."

"Who's Big Tim?"

"He's a man I hired to help with the sheering, he knows about sheep."

Then Dean said, "And he's the best Indian tracker in Mexico he tracked Jim and me across half of Mexico he knows Jim's horse tracks."

Tom said, "Then let's go find Big Tim."

Gary said, 'I'm going to."

They got saddled and were off to get Big Tim along the stream. As they rode up Big Tim came out of their tent eating a chicken leg.

Dean said, "Big Tim, we think Jim might be in some kind of trouble. He's with Tom's daughter Shelly since this morning. We need you to track his horse."

"I know his horse good, track him long way. I get my horse, tell wife."

As Big Tim went inside he threw down the chicken leg.

"Tom said, "I don't know what Jim did to get that big man on his trail but I sure wouldn't want him mad at me."

"Don't worry they're good friends now. Jim got him this job."

Big Tim came out and got his horse saddled and they were off with Tom in the lead all the way to his ranch. They rode up in front of Tom's ranch house and Betty came out on the porch. Big Tim got off his horse and started looking around.

"I see Jim's horse and this must be girl horse less weight. I can follow we find."

Tom said to Betty, "Don't worry, he's an expert tracker."

"Hope find before dark or will have to wait till morning. I not good to track in dark."

"Wait, I'll get you some food in case you are gone overnight."

Betty came out with two big bundles of canvas and we got them tied on three horses and then Big Tim led the way watching the tracks. He moved faster than we thought he would. Then he stopped at the edge of a rock wall.

"Look, turned here to the north. He has to be looking for something cause see here, he's getting off and pulling at the brush against this wall."

Big Tim turned north and slowed down to take his time and the sun was now down and Big Tim stopped.

"Jim looking for something that is in the brush against the rocks. To dark now we find in morning. Easy to track they not trying to hide so no one on their trail this is good. Do not worry we find."

*****

I could see out a window in the now dark room and it was almost dark outside. I had worked the ropes loose enough to reach half way to my boots. I had to keep trying.

"What are you doing Jim?"

"I'm trying to get these ropes a little looser so I can reach my spurs and can cut the ropes. It's going to be harder in the dark. Don't worry we'll get out of here and Tom is out there somewhere."

Then the door opened as we heard steps. Jimmy came in with a lit lantern and set it on the table.

"We're ready to go and this is going to look like an accident."

"I guess that John is going to meet you at Marfa." I said.

"That old fool, he's nothing, just kept us informed of things for a little cash for that dumb wife of his."

"Now Lola and Chance, they will want a piece of the action."

"They were never with us. They just wanted the gold they heard was in the mountains somewhere. We laughed every time they went looking for that gold."

"We know how to get it and we're heading that way tonight. But in an hour or so you two will be dead."

He set the lit lantern on the edge of the table where it was teetering. When it falls it would burst into flames. He then left the room and shut the door. We heard the buggy as the three of them left down the road.

"What are we going to do?"

"Don't worry the ropes are loose enough. We have to get to the ranch and get Dean and head to Marfa. June is in lots of danger."

"And we're not."

By raising my foot and reaching down I could barely reach the buckle that held my spurs in place on my boot. I got it unbuckled and worked the rowel end of the spurs up to the rope and started cutting into the rope that held me to the chair. Just as the strands of rope began to unravel the lantern fell off the table and burst in flames. The ropes came off easily and as the flames caught the bed and curtains on fire I was in back of Shelly untying her hands.

"Hurry, Jim we need to get out of here."

Shelly's hands came loose and we were to the window pulling down the burning curtains as the flames reached the roof of the cabin.

The window was stuck as Shelly held on to my arm so I grabbed a chair next to the bed, which was all in flames now and spreading toward us, and I threw the chair breaking the glass. I picked up Shelly and placed her feet first out the window.

"Get away from here before the roof caves in."

"Hurry Jim jump out."

That's when the window in front of me burst in flames. I had no choice but to back up and take a running leap out the window. I hit the ground rolling over and over trying to put the flames out that had my sleeve on fire. Shelly ran up to me and was throwing dirt all over my shirt. We finally got the fire on my sleeve put out. We stood there holding each other close watching as the cabin went up in flames and the night sky was full of fire and ashes. Some of the pine trees caught fire but that didn't last long as the trees fell into the stream and the fire was put out. The cabin was burned to the ground. We stayed close to the burned out cabin for it was too dark to make our way to where the horses were tied and a night chill was in the air. So we just sit there huddled together till daybreak. All the men seem to have also left. At least they didn't take my gun.

* * * * *

Big Tim was up and was looking to the north when Dean walked up.

"Look at the fire in the sky. Get all up and go. Big trouble over there about five miles."

It was still pretty much dark first light had not peeked over the horizon yet but we were right behind Big Tim as he rode to the north looking at the glow in the sky instead of the ground for tracks. It was slowly becoming lighter when Big Tim stopped and got off his horse.

"Dean, look all tracks, one buggy and three horses. See came out of wall of rock and much brush. Has to open here somewhere. Everyone search for place go through."

We all dismounted and started looking for a way to get through the rock.

* * * * *

Daybreak was upon us and Shelly and me made our way to where Red and her horse were tied. When we reached the spot the horses was gone. The fire must have frightened them and they had pulled away from the brush. I whistled for Red as we made our way to the road and I kept whistling till Red came running up with Shelly's horse on his tail. It felt good to have our horses under us again as we rode toward the outside world. Just as we reached the wall, it started to move and I drew my gun and Shelly got off the road back in the brush. As I pointed my gun at a figure coming through the opening to my amazement it was Big Tim. I yelled,

"Come on in boys, glad to see you. Come on out Shelly its friends."

When Shelly came out of the brush Tom saw her as he passed the wall to the inside. He rushed to her and they leaned out of their saddles and hugged each other.

"Your mother had a feeling yesterday that something was wrong so I went to Gary's and then I met Big Tim, a great tracker, we headed this way and we saw the fire but couldn't find a way through the wall. I'm glad you're safe."

"Thanks to Jim here. They had us tied up and started the fire and Jim got us loose and we went out the window. His arm got burned."

"It's nothing, right now we have more important things. Dean, Jimmy Johnson and Mary Whasworth are heading to Marfa to get June and make her tell them where the gold is. I want you and Big Tim to head that way and stop them. I'm going to go to town and get John to help."

Gary asked, "Jimmy Johnson, isn't he the one that was Sheriff in Marfa."

"Yes, he's the one that killed June's grandfather and Joe. Mary killed Sid. It's a long story. Right now we have to get them from hurting June."

Dean said, "I'm leaving right now." Gary put in.

"I'm going we can stop at the ranch and get some grub. Big Tim you have a permanent job with me. You're wonders with the sheep."

"Go now with you and Dean."

"Shelly, you go home I'm going to help our friends. It's like old times."

"Not on your life dad. June may need some caring for after this is done."

"Gary, when we get to your ranch can Sara go tell Betty that Shelly is fine and what we're doing."

"Sure, Bonnie will want to go to."

"Let's head out I'll be there as quick as I can with or without John."

I lit out for town; Red was ready for the hard run. I looked back and Dean and the others were gone for the ranch and then Marfa. The three in a buggy would be slower than the men on horseback so that would give Dean the edge. As I rode into Alpine it was still early so I rode up to John's house and knocked.

"Who is it? Can't it wait till I'm in the office?"

"John, it's Jim and it can't wait."

John opened the door and I explained some of what happened as he got dressed.

"I can't believe that Jimmy went bad and Mary I trusted."

"She admitted that she was using you, Lola and Chance to get information out of."

"Let's go Jim. It's time to get my self-esteem back I know what you must think of me."

I said as we headed to the livery. "Forget that now, we have a long way to go. As long as you're with us now."

We were on the road to Marfa. We by-passed the ranches and headed west as the sun was already up high in the sky. We were riding at a good pace but the horses couldn't keep going like this so we stopped at the next little creek we came to.

"John, I couldn't tell you everything but I was sent to investigate a murder in Marfa. You know June at the dance it was her grandfather that was murdered and he did find gold and that's what it's all about. Even Lola and Chance have been looking for the gold but Mary was using them to."

We rode on and Red was ready for the run. He always seemed to know when it was time to catch the outlaws. I guess it was in his blood as it has always been in mine. The sun was at our backs as the sweat was rolling down my neck and on my back. There were snakes, lizards, roadrunners and even one lonely coyote that got out of our way as we passed. I could now make out our men's tracks over the buggy tracks. Big Tim was having no trouble following the tracks. I could tell that they were only an hour ahead of us and they were only an hour behind Jimmy and Mary. It was now late afternoon and the sun wouldn't give up its heat. The heat radiated off everything in the desert my canteen was almost empty as we came to another creek. This one barely had water in it and it wasn't very good water. But even bad water is better than no water. It meant the difference between life and death. There were always animals and buzzards ready to pick the bones clean of anyone that ran out of water and didn't make it to the next town. It was finally starting to cool off a little as the sun started its trek behind the western mountains. As we took a rest John fixed some coffee.

"You know what? The other day Todd and Maggie dropped by and told me that when they saw June at the dance it reminded them of when they had a store in Marfa so after the dance they rode over there. They said it was clean as a whistle and they're thinking of opening another store over here if more people come in."

"Dean saw them coming from Marfa and we thought that they might be involved with the murders."

John laughed as he shook his head, "Those two no way. They just think about getting ahead in life the honest way."

"We were watching everyone close."

We went on and dark came on us now and the moon wasn't out so it was slow going. We would be there in an hour or so if we kept at this pace. The others would be there now and I hoped that Jimmy couldn't find June. He might kill her if she didn't tell him where the gold was and if she did he would sure do her in. As we came down main street everything was quiet almost to quiet. There were no lights anywhere and the only sound was the clip, clap of our horse's hoofs as we tied up behind the general store. I had one advantage over the others, Dean and I had spent time in this ghost town. There must be more people in Marfa now than in the last ten years. I led John into the general store and nobody. I was sure June knew that all these people were here. She would know Dean and Shelly as her friends.

"Let's see who might had left their horses in the stable."

As we moved slowly toward the stable I looked in most of the buildings. They were all dark inside.

"I wonder where they are?'

"We'll find them and I know if June is around she will know that everyone is in town. She usually finds me before I know she's around."

The stable had a buggy and two horses which were still harnessed to the buggy but no other sign of life. Then out of the silent of the night came a loud yell as if someone in pain.

I asked, "John, which way did that come from?"

"Sounds like from down to the east."

"Must be the saloon."

We worked our way along the walls of the building on the boardwalks. I pushed open the bat-winged door of the saloon before we went in and there was another scream and it was in the saloon all right so John and me went carefully through the door. We worked our way to the stairs and another scream. We were on the right track the scream came from upstairs. As we reached the top of the stairs I turned to go down the corridor and as I passed the first room a large hand reached out and grabbed my shoulder. I turned and there was Big Tim.

"Big Tim you scared the daylights out of me. John, this is Big Tim he works for Gary. What's going on with the screams?"

John said, "I'm glad he's on our side."

"I stand guard, woman have baby. The other two left her here. Tom's daughter with her told me to keep men out."

"Where are Dean, Tom and Gary?"

"They looking for the man and the woman that left woman having baby, think Dean wants to find June."

"We'll go find them. This woman we're looking for wants that baby so if she comes back grab her. Be careful, she's already killed one man."

There was another scream as we made our way back down the dark stairs. As we went out the bat-winged doors I saw a shadow coming toward me it was Tom.

"Tom, it's John and me, where's Gary and Dean."

"They're still looking, I came back to check on Shelly."

"She's fine, Big Tim's there. Nothing is going to get passed him. The baby hasn't come yet."

"I think that all the ghost in town knows that." He chuckled.

"I'll go with you. Dean is trying to find a secret room that June took him to but he said it was daylight when he went there before."

"There's no sign of Mary or Jimmy."

"No, and that's what Dean's worried about with June missing."

"I don't know even where she stays. Guy, her grandfather and her have been around here for years. I don't even know where the mine is located. I know that she has boo-be traps all over."

I led the way to the hotel where I first laid eyes on her and it was night like this. I pushed open the door and we rushed in and a shot went over our heads and we hit the floor with our guns out.

"It came from up there; I'm going up you two cover me and watch for someone coming down. There's a back way out but they may not know about it."

I started up the stairs and another shot rang out with my gun answering it. I heard a noise behind me and saw Dean and Gary come in the door. I worked up the stairs till I reached the top. I started checking each room. I yelled for them to come on up.

"They're gone and June is with them."

Dean looked at the room I found and there were signs of three people and there were some ropes left tied to the bed.

"They got her."

"Don't worry Dean we'll find her."

"Gary, Tom will you two go take Big Tim's place at the saloon I'm going to need him to track them when daylight comes. Be very careful cause Mary wants that baby and she's a killer and she doesn't care for Stella at all. She may even try to kill her before she takes the baby."

They left and we waited for Big Tim. It has been a long night but I could see the first sign of the suns light coming up in the east. There had been no more screams for a while, that could mean that the baby was here and Mary would know that to. Big Tim came up the stairs as quiet as if he was in the woods. By now the light was coming through the window. He looked around the room and looked at the ropes. Then he looked at us.

"Light enough I can follow. Girl die baby alive! Gary and Tom with his daughter and baby boy. Will stay there to protect the two."

We left the hotel by the back stairs and toward the stables. Big Tim looked around and found a strand of rope.

"This is right rope but no trail. Like wall of rock hidden."

"Everyone, look around for a trap door anywhere."

Their searched continued and there was no sign then Dean went to the storage room at the far end of the barn. He called to us. When we went in Dean was knocking on the wall and rubbing his hands across it.

"Listen it's hollow behind there. There must be a way in through this wall."

We started feeling and pushing against the wall and nothing. Then I felt a loose board at the bottom of the wall. I pulled outward on it and the wall started to move. There in front of us was stairs going down at least thirty feet under the surface of the stable. When we hit the bottom there were lit lantern down four or five tunnels. They were wide enough for wagons and horses. Each tunnel had a sign saying where it lead. Big Tim looked around and took the tunnel with no sign.

"Hurry, girl this way. Three go in this way; look only two come out one man and one woman bigger than girl. They go that way."

I looked up and the sign said, "to east of town". Then a shot rang out and then another and another the bullets ricocheted off the rock walls of the tunnels and we hit the ground. The shooting stopped and we headed down the tunnel with no name. We came to a door and it was open.

12

This must be her home for we were standing in what would be a front room and to the left there was a doorway that lead to a kitchen. Then we heard sounds coming from in back of the front room. There lying on a bed was June and she had been beaten and her clothes torn. Her eyes were near swollen shut and she had cuts all over her body that we could see. Dean rushed to her and when she saw him through her swollen eyes she started to cry and he took her in his arms.

"You're alright now, we'll get them. They'll pay for this."

"Jim, I didn't tell where the mine is. Gold ore also hidden"

"Don't worry about that now."

"They left when they heard you coming. Said going to try to make the train in Alpine."

"Dean, you take June to Shelly and get her and the baby to the ranch and get the doc, we're going after them. They went to the "out of town tunnel" so they left the buggy in the stable use that to get them back to the ranch."

June barely spoke, "Jim, horses at the end of that tunnel for them to take."

Big Tim led the way and as we went down the "out of town" tunnel I saw Dean carrying the battered body of June up the stairs to the stable. We rushed down the tunnel that seemed to go on and on. At the end of this tunnel was stairs that looked to be fifty feet up to the top. It was like the other door we had to find the key to open it.

It wasn't at the bottom like the other. I searched one side and John the other.

"Here it is."

John said as he pulled up on what looked like a lever. As he pulled up on the lever about three feet of the wall started to rise. When we were outside we found the lever on this side and closed the door.

"Big Tim, our horses are over here."

"Mine near."

As we left town down Main Street I saw Dean carrying June to the stables with Sherry carrying the baby and Gary and Tom not far behind searching with their eyes the whole area with their guns drawn and ready for action. We would have to come back and bury Stella when this was over. I turned my attention to the problem at hand. We had to make that train before it left. I rode up beside John. Big Tim was having no problem with the trail it was in plain sight.

"John, when does the train pull out?"

"There's one tomorrow morning. If it's on time it pulls out at 10:30 AM."

"We need to ride straight through the night. Only stop to give the horses a breather and water."

We rode on through the desert land that had life and death in its depths. The blazing sun was well up in the sky now and the heat was intense as we came to the first water. There was not much water but enough for the horses and us to fill our canteens. I saw Big Tim pouring water all down his shirt and pants. He looked at me.

"Take sun away, make me cool for hour or two."

I did the same and then John got the idea. It did take the heat away. Then we were off and after our clothes dried out the sun became nearly unbearable. It was well in the afternoon before we found water again. Our canteens were empty and I knew the horses were drier than we were. We stayed an hour letting the horses get water more than once and to chomp on the nearby grass and that was only grass near because of the water. Big Tim spoke out.

"Can tell they not take care of horses. Not stop for water. Horses not last. We take time to care horses. Catch tomorrow, they slow down."

The sun was down in the west only the rays of the sun were showing over the mountain and we kept to the trail. To my delight the half-moon rose early to give us some light to move through the desert better. We stopped at the next water hole and while the horses were grazing and watering I built a small fire and cooked some eggs and bacon.

"Good Jim. Help us make it."

John said, "Big Tim after this is over can I call on you to help me track if I need you. I will make you a part-time deputy and pay you."

"First job, sheep. Sure Mr. Thomas let me help you when you need Big Tim. Will be good."

"Alright, it will be good. Thank you."

We put out the fire and were off into the dark night. All through the night we moved for it was a lot cooler and the horses regained some of their strength with that coolness.

* * * * *

Shelly had got in the back seat of the buggy where Dean had lay June. The baby was in front with Dean. Dean had filled an empty whiskey bottle with water and found some clean rags for Shelly to bathe June's cuts. He took a full whiskey bottle cause they had no milk for the baby. Dean thought a little whiskey mixed with water would keep the boy alive till they could get some milk. Tom and Gary were riding behind with Shelly and Dean's horses tied to the back of the buggy. Shade was hard to come by in the heat of the day but the baby slept with a blanket covering him and June was in severe pain with the bouncing of the buggy. Dean followed the way Big

Tim was taking Jim and came to the same water holes that they did. Dean would take June down and Shelly would get some fresh water to bathe her and just let the baby suck on a rag soaked with water and whiskey. Tom and Gary would rustle up some food.

Shelly said, "Dean, I'm worried about some of June's cuts they are starting to look red."

Tom spoke out, "Shelly, take a rag and soak it in that whiskey and bathe them with that. It will burn and hurt her for a moment but it will stop any infection that has started."

They ate and was on the way again and it was night when they stopped again. Gary came over.

"Dean, Shelly do you think we should rest till morning or lite out through the night. Can June and the baby take it."

"Dean, I think we should keep moving. I won't sleep if we stay here and June seems to be in less pain now and might get as much sleep moving as staying here."

"Let's keep moving, the sooner we get her to the ranch the better, then I'll go to town and get doc."

Tom said, "Then Gary and me will move out in front to see any trouble coming."

They moved out and the baby seemed to be holding its own and June seemed to be resting better.

* * * * *

The first rays of the sun hit me right in the eyes and woke me up. I guess I had fallen asleep in the saddle. Big Tim was still in the lead and I could feel with my legs that Red was tired real tired. We stopped at a water hole and I nearly fell on the ground. Big Tim said. "Last water hole before town and they not stop for water. Will find horses soon."

"You saying there horses will be dead."

"Strong horses, I thought dead before now. Girl must take good care of her animals. I have canvas bags will fill with water. We give their horses if we find alive. If can, they will follow. Thomas will find and take to ranch."

"How you know that?"

"Saw fire last night on back trail. Must be them."

We ate some dry jerky and rested as the horses watered and ate some grass. Within two miles we found one horse down but alive. We striped the saddle off and Big Tim gave it some water and he still had signs of life.

"Only five miles to town. You know way I stay and take care of horse for girl. Too good to die this close to ranch, Thomas be here soon. Think you can handle those two."

We were up on our horses and gone in a minute. I turned and saw that Big Tim had the horse on its feet. Jimmy and Mary were now on one horse and it was 9:00. The train would leave in one and a half hours. We passed the road leading to the ranch and headed on to town. I could tell from the deep tracks that the horse was struggling to stay up. But the two pushed him on. We came around a set of boulders on each side of the road and knew that Alpine was not far off. It was 10:15 when we came to the edge of town. There in front of the livery we saw the horse down and Jeb was with it with some water. As we passed him I yelled.

"Take care of that horse."

"They went to the train; I can't stand anyone treating an animal like this. I'll do everything I can."

As we approached the train it was pulling out of the station and we could see the two just getting to their seats in the passenger car. They saw us, and that's when Jimmy headed to the back of the car. I yelled to John.

"Let's catch that train. You get Mary and I'll get Jimmy. I know you're tired Red but we have to catch that train and then you can rest for a week. John don't take that woman lightly she's dangerous."

We had to race for the train and it was moving away a little. Then Red had a burst of speed and I got hold of the rail on the caboose and pulled myself on board and Red dropped back and John's horse was coming on strong and I put out a hand to John and he grabbed it and swung a board.

"That was close." John said.

"You go get Mary and I'll find Jimmy."

I looked back as we rushed through the caboose and Red and John's horse were heading back to town stopping to eat the grass along the track.

As we came to the door of the caboose and started to open it a shot hit right above my hat. Jimmy was in the next car.

"You keep him busy; I'm going up and over. I'll draw him to me and you go get Mary."

I went to the back of the train and climbed the ladder to the top of the train. The wind was strong in my face. As I worked my way along the top the wind caught my hat and sent it sailing off my head. Jimmy must have seen it fly off for he was up the ladder on the front end of the caboose. As he came over the edge to the top I saw him and drew my gun and fired at him. I was now flat on my stomach inching toward him. He shot at me and was moving my way. I took another shot and he laid flat against the roof of the train as he moved forward and tried another shot and missed. I took that time and stood up to rush him and grabbed his gun hand as he started to squeeze off another shot then his gun when flying over the side of the train. As we fought I heard shooting coming from the passenger car. He hit me a good blow to the left side of my head that sent me falling to the side of the roof. I caught my balance before I went over the side then I was in his face again and struck him in the nose and it broke and blood went all over us then I hit him in the stomach. This sent him flying back falling and hitting his head on a pipe sticking up out of the roof. He was up and on me again and this time the blow hit me in the mouth and blood went flying all over and sent me flying over the edge of the roof. I caught the edge and started pulling myself up when Jimmy started stomping on my hand. That made me let go and I was hanging by one hand as he started to stomp on my other hand. I saw it coming but Jimmy didn't and the edge of the train tunnel caught him on the side of his head. I got a good hold and pulled myself back on the roof of the train. I laid flat till the train was out of the tunnel and I saw that Jimmy was lying flat on his back. I turned my back on Jimmy as I saw John coming up the ladder. That's when Jimmy grabbed my gun and I turned toward him and as he pointed my gun at me and started to pull the trigger I heard a shot and my gun fell to the roof of the train and Jimmy stumbled and fell over the edge of the train and I saw him hit a broken dead tree and he was impounded on it ten feet up in the air. I went over and picked up my gun and walked over to John and we started down the ladder. "Thanks John he had me cold and I knew there was one more shell in my gun."

"Just part of the job."

"What happened down there? I heard a shot."

"Mary said she didn't want to live without her baby or the gold and go to prison so right there in front of the passengers she put the gun to her head and pulled the trigger. She died right there in her seat. I took her body to the baggage car."

The train came to a slow stop and then started backing up to town. The engineer stopped at the dead tree and John and me managed to get Jimmy off the dead tree. We put his body in the baggage car next to Mary's. When we got to town I saw that Jeb had rounded up Red and John's horse and was going into the stables. We unloaded the bodies and the train left town for the second time today. John had some men take the two bodies to the undertakers and John went to his office and I went to the telegraph office and sent a wire.

To Captain Turbrough:

Caught two murderers both dead. Jimmy Johnson ex-sheriff Of Marfa, Texas killed by present Sheriff of Alpine, John Brady saved my life. Second murderer was a woman, Mary Whasworth, she shot herself in front of passengers on the train. Just a few loose ends to finish up and I request a month off. This was a tough case.

Texas Ranger Jim Beddly

I took a copy to John and he read it.

"Thanks Jim for not mentioning all the trouble I caused."

"Just doing my job. We all make little mistakes time to time. If you need me I'll be at Gary shearing sheep."

I was walking to the stable when Gerald ran up to me.

"Here's your answer."

I opened it and read.

Good work Jim, now it's time for another case.
But take that month off you and Red earned it.

Your Captain
John Turbrough

I had to laugh a little to myself and looked up and saw the Long Bar. I decided that I needed a beer. I got my beer from Doby and saw Lola and Chance playing cards. So I went over and sat to drink my beer.

"Hello Jim." Lola said.

"You two nearly got killed. Just hunt for your own gold and don't hire any more gunmen. You two have a good business here. Stay clear of trouble and you won't be seeing much of me. Just time to time for a nice friendly beer. I do like that bar and its namesake. I don't know for sure who killed Ted but I think it was Mary. By the way, Stella that worked for you died giving birth to a little boy yesterday. He's out at Gary's. Shelly is taking care of him."

I drank up my beer and walked out to get Red. Jeb was rubbing down the horse of June's when I walked in. He said.

"Strong horse, it will take a couple of days to get him back to normal but Red is ready to go. That horse of yours and John's are the best."

"We stopped at every water hole and let them drink and eat grass. We knew that Jimmy and Mary would run June's two horses into the ground. They left the other one out on the trail nearly dead. Big Tim took it to Gray's ranch."

"I just can't believe that Mary was a murderer. Lived right here with us. Who did she kill?"

"She admitted to killing her Sid. But I think she killed Ted at the dance. I better see how things are going with June at Gary's. They beat her pretty good."

I saddled Red and headed to the ranch. Todd stopped me in the street.

"Is it true what I heard about over in Marfa. That girl found a gold mine. If so we're opening a second store over there."

"I think she will have to get well first and then she just might want to talk about that. June has kept it in good shape."

"I saw that, Maggie and me were over there after the dance when we saw June. We remembered her and Guy over in Marfa before the railroad came here."

I rode Red out of town at a slow pace. He'd been through a lot these pass two days. I saw the doc coming back to town from the ranch. I stopped and he pulled up beside me and stopped.

"How's June and the baby?"

"June has some deep cuts but they will heal in a month or so. I don't think they will leave any scars. Tom helped save her on the way back by pouring whiskey on the cuts. Kept them from getting infected. The baby is strong and he's taken to the goat milk. That was Gary's idea and a good one. I'll be back out in three or four days. Any trouble come a running."

"Thanks doc."

I went a little further and Dean came racing up.

"Where the fire Dean?"

"No fire was coming to help you. Big Tim said you two could handle trouble."

"We did and the trouble is gone now. June can open her mine after she files on it and get a real mine going. No more hiding out in those tunnels but they can be handy."

"You heading for the ranch."

"Sure thing, just taken my time. Red is as tucked as I am. I promised him a week's rest."

"You know the sheep shearing is in three days."

"Captain gave me a month off so I'll be here. How's June fairin'?"

"Good, doc says she'll be like new in three or four weeks."

"That's good. You know Dean one thing has me puzzled, when Jimmy tried to burn us in that house there were three men riding in there for him. I think they're the ones that hit me over the head. Where did they go?"

"Could be they just skedaddled."

"I wish I knew."

We rode up to the house and Shelly and Tom came out. I jumped off Red and Shelly came into my arms and I kissed her.

"You two beat all, first she shoots at you and now she's kissing you." Tom let out a laugh.

"Dad! Are you alright Jim?"

"Shelly, he looks fine."

"Sir, I am. Tom before I forget, you know back where y'all found us. Back pass the burned out cabin there is a pasture that has lots of your branded cattle that Jimmy just happen to have."

"I'll send some boys over there to get them. Thanks Jim."

"Now Shelly, led me to that girl that started all this. Dean, come on in I'm sure you don't mind seeing June again."

We went into the house and there in the same bed that I had recovered was June. She put out her hand and I gave her mine. Shelly said.

"I'll let you three talk about the case. I'll see if Bonnie will let me fix you some breakfast. I'm sure you're hungry after the ride."

"Sure am. Now June I got your grandfather's killer it was that Jimmy Johnson. He's dead and so is Mary. She shot herself. I'm just sorry I wasn't there to stop them before they did this to you."

"Jim, I don't blame you. It would be impossible for you or Dean to be everywhere to stop all the evil people. It was Mary that did most of this after I wouldn't tell Johnson anything. She was insane with the thought of that gold and baby. To her nothing else mattered."

"You are so good at hiding how did they find you."

"It was this one's fault." She took Dean's hand.

"Just like you told us not to do I was sitting in the hotel thinking about Dean and they grabbed me from the back. It was as simple as that. I led them to my house below so they would stop hitting me. I knew that they still wouldn't fine the gold or the mine from down there."

"Where is the mine? You can now file a legal claim on it."

"When I'm well I'll show you. Dean would you hire someone to go down to the tunnels and the one in the barn. All my animals are down there they need water and food and there's a way to bring the animals up to the surface. It's under the hay in the corral."

"I'll take care of it. Who did all the tunnel work down there?"

"Mostly Grandfather before I came to live with him. I did mostly around the house area and I finished the tunnel that led to the mine and where I have a stock pile of ore stored."

"We'll let you get some sleep so you can get well."

Dean kissed her and we left to eat breakfast. As we were sitting there I looked up at Tom.

"You know Tom, I want to go in there and help your men with the cattle."

"Change your mind about working for me."

Gary looked up at me with a frown on his face.

"No, there were three men in the valley helping Jimmy Johnson and I don't know where they went. I just want to make sure they left the country."

"You're welcomed to come along."

"I'm going to." Shelly said.

"I don't think that's a good idea."

'Well I do they helped tie me up and knock you out."

"Jim, you might as well face it. There's not much that this girl will change her mind on."

"Alright but you get out of the way if need be. Dean you come to if you will. We can be on the lookout while they drive the cattle out of there. First I'm going to sleep for a day or so."

Shelly got up and went to the other room and came back out with a bundle and uncovered a small baby.

"I'll be, near forget about him. How's he doing?"

"Take's to this goats milk like his own mothers. Poor girl. I do feel for her. I just wish she could have seen what good she brought into this world."

"Dean, that's another thing whoever you send please bury that girl. I wish we had had time. What you going to call him?"

"I thought we could name him together."

"I'll think on it. I need to get some sleep now."

Dean and me went to the bunkhouse but before we got there Big Tim came over.

"Horse will be good. Strong to take that bad treatment and girl can ride home when well."

"Big Tim the other horse is in town. The man at the livery said the same thing. This is good."

I was out like a log by the time my head hit the pillow. I woke up once before dark and Pickin's was sitting on his bunk looking at me.

"Haven't seen much of you. 'Bout time you come in and earn your keep."

I pulled the cover over my head and turned over and went back to sleep. When I woke it must had been morning cause the sun was out and Pickin's wasn't there. I looked over and Dean was gone. So I got up and got my clothes and guns on and headed to the house.

To my surprise June was sitting up eating some breakfast with Shelly. I sat down and Shelly brought me a plate."

"Thank you Shelly. Glad to see you up June and eating. Where is everyone? I thought you would be gone Shelly."

"I'm helping Bonnie and Sara with June and the baby. We take turns with the baby and cooking. That boy takes looking after twenty-four hours a day. Gary's men are bringing the sheep in for the shearing day after tomorrow."

"That's right, just too much has happened."

"My dad and the men are getting ready to go get those cattle. It's about Sara's turn so we can head out and meet my dad about 10:00 at the so-called gate."

"We had better get a move on. See you later June we'll talk more."

Sara came in and Shelly and me went to the barn and saddled up and were off down the trail and as we were riding Shelly looked over at me.

"Jim, after this what are you going to do."

"I have a month off but after that I'm not for sure. I like it around here and the people are the best once you get to know them and can keep the young ladies from shooting at you."

"Now Jim you know why I did that. I'm just glad I didn't kill you. I wouldn't have known how good you are. Now I'm wondering who took that shot at me and why."

"Thank you young lady for not being a better shot and we might never know who took that shot and I've also been thinking about that land that we are coming to. I've been thinking about looking into buying it if I can. It's so beautiful and a place I can come when my Ranger days are over."

"That would be so great if you did that. We would be neighbors and good friends."

"That's the idea, but I think of you as a little more than a friend."

She didn't have time to response cause Tom and two of his men were riding up to us and Dean came up from behind us.

"You nearly left me behind." Dean said.

"Howdy, Jim, did you get some beauty sleep." Then Tom laughed.

"I'm looking forward to this and a month off to look around this place."

"Dad, he's thinking about buying this land back in here."

"Why I didn't even know this place existed a week ago or I would might have bought it. Having you for a friend and neighbor will be good."

We went up to the rock face and I reached in and pulled up the rock and brush and we went in and headed down the road.

"You told your men to watch for the three men I told you about? Dean and me will watch your backs while you get the cattle together and head them out."

We rode up to the burned out house and stopped and looked at it.

"Jim, is this where you and Shelly were tied up."

"Yes and we just barely made it out. It got pretty hot in there and I'm glad I had another shirt the one I had on was burned and black as night. Just glad it didn't get to the skin to bad. That's one thing I don't know if I could forget about that night and nearly losing Shelly."

"Jim, I could forget it and so can you. Just get rid of all this rubble and build a big, nice house with a barn over there."

"Alright you two which way to the cattle."

"Anywhere from here to the south about a mile. There's pastures back pass those cedars over yonder."

They headed out and Dean and me with Shelly alongside of us kept in back of them. As we broke out of the tall trees the sight was something to behold.

"My Lord, Jim I forgot the beauty of this place and look at all the cattle. They are dad's look at the brand." As Tom and his men herded the cattle toward the road out, Tom came over.

"Should have brought more men. I thought you said a few. I think I'll have more than I lost with all the yearlings and calves that are here. They're not even branded. Johnson was kind of dumb he had a gold mine right here in the walls of this valley. If he would have bought cattle instead of stealing them."

"Bad men are never smart."

"Boss, over here what do we do with these."

We rode over and there were about two hundred sheep. I said.

"Leave them I've found out that it takes dogs to handle them right. Gary will bring his dogs and get them."

There was a clicking sound behind us. Everyone froze for a minute. As I started to turn I motioned for Shelly to get off to the side by her dad. She moved her horse and Dean and me were looking at three men.

13

"What you think you is going with our cattle? You could get hung for that."

"I know and I'll be the one doing the hanging if any is to be done."

I said as I pulled back my vest a little to let my badge show.

"These cattle are this man's they have his brand on them and the calves belong to his cows. So just move along your boss won't be coming back ever."

They looked at each other and I made a sign to Dean to get ready. My eyes were looking right into theirs as they pulled their guns but mine and Deans was already out and the look in their eyes was of shock and we squeezed our triggers and the bullets hit them square in the chest and they fell out of their saddles dead on the ground.

"Tom, get your cattle out of here. I think that was all of his men but I'm not for sure. Dean and me will take these three to John; I'll let him do the paperwork. Shelly, you go with your dad I'll see you later and we'll talk more. I'll tell Gary about the sheep on the way to town."

We got the three slung across their horses and we followed the cattle and Tom's men out the gate. We stopped and told Bonnie to tell Gary about the sheep and we went to town. We stopped in front of John's office. John came out and looked at each body.

"What you doing Jim trying to clean up the country by yourself?"

"Had some help I think this fella beside me is faster than I am."

"Come on Jim, you got two of them."

"Now that could be argued."

"Just take them to the undertaker and tell Bill to sell their things to pay for burial."

"Now what happen, I'll have to write a report."

"Better you than me. Tom and two of his men with Dean and Shelly and me went into Jimmy's valley to get his branded cattle and their calf's and these three are the one that slugged me and tied Shelly and me up two days ago. Anyway, they tried to stop us and they lost."

"Well you have a passel of witnesses. I believe two of them were wanted who get the reward."

"You know as a Ranger I can't take rewards. Give it to Dean here."

"What me?"

"Sure, you got two of them anyway.

"Now Jim."

We dropped our packages off at the undertakers.

"Jim, I better get back and help Gary."

"I'll be a while."

I went to the assayer office and talked to the clerk. He gave me an application for June to fill out and a map where the mine is located. I tucked it in my shirtfront and headed to the land office. Jerry said.

"Where is this land that you're talking about? Here show me on the map."

"Right here where this line starts on the west right up against Tom Davis ranch and over here to the east, haven't been over there yet, and up here north, haven't been up there either and down here to the main road coming from the east to Alpine. It's that whole blank space on the map."

"There's a good reason it's blank."

"Someone owns it?"

"No, it's blank cause no one has ever tried to claim it. Let's see it seems to be about four miles from east to west and with a little indention up here could be five miles from north to south that's about twenty square miles or so. I'll have to send a survey crew out that way to set the boundaries for you and then we'll know for sure. I'll have to charge you a survey fee of one-hundred dollars since it's never been surveyed before and the registration fee of forty dollars. That's a total of one hundred and forty dollars in cash. Now whom do I make the title out to."

"What are you saying?"

"You pay me the fee and I make out the deed in who's ever name you want."

"It's mine."

"Once you give me the cash. Then you get the deed after the survey is complete and is registered in the name you choose."

"Then put in Mr. and Mrs. Jim Beddly. Here's the money,"

"I hadn't heard you were married."

"I'm not yet. But will be some day. It's a little hard to get in there but you enter on the west about here on the map. I'll leave the gate open."

"After the survey is done I'll send the deed out to you. You still at Gary Thomas's ranch."

"Sure thing."

I stuck another piece of paper in my shirt and headed to the ranch with a smile on my face. I just hoped that Shelly liked it. When I rode up I had a large smile still on my face and Shelly was standing on the front porch.

"What is wrong with you Jim? What's with that big grin on your face?"

"Can't say right now. Maybe in a couple of days."

I went in to see June and sat down and told her.

"I went to the assayer's office while I was in town and got these papers for you to look at while you have time. There's a map for you to mark it on. I know how you feel about letting everyone know where the mine is. This way if someone tries to take the mine from you you'll have something to take to court. If you want to enjoy what you and Guy worked for then you're going to have to hire people to work for you."

"It's hard we had to hide it for so many years and then when grandfather told people to try to keep them in Marfa he was killed. But I'm tired of the secrets and hiding. I'll look over the papers and maybe fill them out."

"When you're better we'll go and get some ore samples. They'll need that to resister the claim."

I went to the front porch and sat down beside Shelly.

"Jim, I've been thinking all day about what you said this morning before we met up with dad. What exactly did you mean?"

"About what?"

"You know that you feel that we are more than friends."

"We are aren't we?"

"I do think so but what did you mean."

"I've been thinking that I have been a Texas Ranger for twelve years now and I'm thirty years old now. I love being a Ranger and helping people like Tom, Gary and June. Good people but it's not a life if one wants to take a wife. Now I may let Cap know if he needs me bad he can call on me once in a while. I don't know how a wife would feel about that."

"She might not mind so much if the case didn't involve a pretty girl like June or a woman like Lola."

"Oh, you know Lola?"

"Yes, I do."

"You need me to take you home tonight."

"No, I'm spending the night to take care of the baby."

"I'm going to be real busy the next two days but I want to tell and ask you something day after tomorrow."

"Alright Jim, I'll be around."

"Goodnight!"

"Goodnight Jim."

The next morning I went out with the men and helped the dogs gather the sheep in closer to the shearing barn. Gary hired four wagons that were sitting by the barn. Big Tim's wife and children would help load the wagons, along with Bonnie, with wool which would be driven to town by Dean, Pickin's and me and one wagon would be left here to load. Sara would be on horseback making sure the dogs were bringing the sheep in when necessary. Shelly was going to look after the baby and June all day. That would leave Gary, Bob, Slim and Big Tim to do the shearing. Gary hired four men to guard the barn in town two during the day and two at night. We didn't think anything would happen till the train came with the boxcars but why take a chance. When the morning came we were ready. After breakfast everyone was in place and the first sheep were let into the barn and I watched in amazement as each man would take a sheep and cut all the wool off in a matter of five minutes or less. Big Tim was the best he could get the job done in three minute even the males. Which was a type of chore. It had to be done carefully or they could lose their manhood and no more lambs from that ram. The sheep were let loose in a separate pasture after they had been sheared so they wouldn't have to kept separating them from the wooly sheep. When the wagons were loaded we headed for town. Some people were out watching as we rolled through Alpine and to the other side of town. Gary had hired three men to bundle up the wool in burlap and tie it tight with wire as we came in. The burlap had been in the loft the night of the dance. The bundles were about fifty pounds each. When the day was over we had only done thirty per cent. Everyone worked so hard that Betty had come over and help Shelly fix a buffet supper outside. Even June had gotten out of bed and helped. She was moving slow but that girl had a will to fight. I had taken the last load for the day and helped the men bundle it up and made sure the guards were on duty before I left for my supper. This went on for four days but we were done.

On the last day at the supper outside, Gary and me were eating and drinking our big glass of tea when Gary called Big Tim over. He came over with his wife and his children.

"Have a seat Big Tim and you Little Fawn, I just want to tell you what a great job you and your family did. You are now one of our family if you want to be."

Big Tim looked at Little Fawn and they both smiled at each other and said;

"Yes" at the same time. Then Little Fawn poked Big Tim in the side and said:

"Now time to ask boss."

"Now we permanent wife wants to have a cabin. I will build in my off time and get trees from around here. Won't cost boss anything. Everyone now please call me Tim no more Big. Families now, do not need to scare anyone anymore. We find place we belong."

"Alright Tim find a nice spot and Little Fawn can have her cabin."

Tim picked up Little Fawn and swung her in the air and she was smiling all the time then the children ran up and hugged both parents.

"Tim, you and your family will get a big bonus."

Then Gary yelled out.

"I've sent a telegram to the broker in Chicago and they have bought all the wool pending on what the inspector says about the quality of the wool when he gets here day after tomorrow. If we get the price we agreed upon everyone will get a bonus." All the hands went wild and were throwing hats in the air and dancing with each other."

When the celebration was over I called Gary to the side. "Gary, you tell me if it's none of my business but how are you getting paid? I can't give up the Ranger in me even if I am on leave for a time."

"I appreciate your concern and it has me a little concerned. With Sid and Mary's death there is no bank. The city fathers took the money that was in the bank and gave it all back to each depositor and what was left over Todd is keeping and he is our banker for now. I trust Todd but I have a lot of money and it will be a temptation if word gets around. The man coming on the train to inspect the wool will have $150,000 with him and he will take some out if the quality is less than expected. I will bring it home."

"That's a temptation alright. You can't take a chance with that much money. I'll be with you and all the men if need be."

"That's what I was hoping for. That many men will draw attention but it can't be helped."

"Tonight and tomorrow night I'm going to get Dean and go to town and watch the guards. I think the wool will be all right they will be after the money. What crook wants to work that hard to take the wool and no place to sell it? They'll wait for the money."

"Thanks Jim, you have been so much help and that two hundred head you found in that valley was a lot of wool."

Dean and me took Shelly and Betty home and I said goodnight to Shelly on the front porch as Tom stood by the front door.

"When you two going to get together for good? Even if he is a part time sheep herder."

"Dad, get inside."

Tom went inside laughing. I kissed her and Dean was already out of the yard when I caught up with him. We were riding side by side into town when Dean came out with.

"Y'all are hitting it off. When you going to marry her."

"I'm working on that right now. I should know by tomorrow."

"What, you can't tell me?"

"I'll tell you after I ask Shelly. Anyway you and June look good together. When are you going to ask her?"

"I don't know, with her owning a gold mine people might talk about me marrying her for the money. Jim, what are we doing in town anyway Gary has guards. I thought we already got rid of all the bad men around these parts."

"Where money shows up the bad men seems to follow. I guess it's the Ranger in me."

We found a hidden place to watch the barn from. We could see the two guards walking around the old barn and would check the lock on the door every time they went around. It was pass midnight and everything looked fine but I had a strange feeling. Dean was yawning and I was feeling a little sleepy.

"Dean, why don't you head to the ranch and get some sleep everything looks fine here. Today was a hard day but tomorrow will be easier. I'll stay a couple more hours and head back."

"Sounds good to me. See you in the morning."

Dean left and within an hour the men had a visitor. It was hard to see who it was but I did see that it was a woman and she was handing them a bottle. I was afraid it was Lola but I couldn't make out her face. They talked for a while and she headed for the Long Bar. I stayed for another hour and went back to the ranch. I was sure some kind of plan was taking shape in their mind. I would see tomorrow night. I had already warned those two.

The next morning I told Gary what had happened and that I was going to spend another night on watch. The train would be in tomorrow morning and all the hands would be in town loading the wool on the train after the final deal was made. Then the train would be off with the agent and the wool but Gary would have the money to take to the ranch. That night I went to town alone and kept watch. It happened at the same time and this time Lola had Chance with her and they stayed for two hours. Now I didn't know who to trust. The men at the ranch I was sure about but here in town I just didn't know anyone I would trust. When they left I went back to the ranch.

I was up extra early and was on Red heading to town. I had woke Dean up and told him to let Gary know that I was already in town and to get there as so as possible. When the train came in the agent would need protection. When I rode through town on the way to the barn I noticed the two night guards were on horseback leaving town. I followed and when they passed the old barn, where the wool was stored, the two daytime guards waved at them as they went by. I stopped and told the guards that Gary was going to be here any time now. As I followed the two guards they took a turn and followed the rail tracks to the east. I looked back and saw Dean coming up fast.

"What's going on?"

"Those two guards that were on guard for the last two night are following the rails to the east. Looks like they're going to meet the train."

"But, what for?"

"We'll see in a while; I hear the train. Look up ahead there's something on the track and one of them is waving a red flag. See over there the other one is in the brush and two more people are there with him."

We watched from a distance and saw as the train came to a stop. Then from the brush came the other guard and riding out on their horses was Lola dress in riding pants and Chance. As we rushed toward the train the four would-be train robbers climbed on board. We had our guns blasting at them and the engineer was clearing off the track and by the time we reached the train he had the train moving. With all the shooting their horses scattered and we caught the train and swung on board. The passengers looked scared as we enter the car and saw the four heading out the back way. The wool agent saw my badge and yelled.

"Ranger, they have the money."

"Dean, head back and go up on top I'll head this way. We'll try to box them in."

As I headed to the back of the car I heard shooting coming from up above. I went through the next car and up the ladder and there was more shooting as I reached the top of the car. I could see Dean two cars away shooting at the four and they were heading back my way as I poked my head above the top of the car. Lola had hold of the money in one hand and a gun in the other. When they saw me the shooting came my way. Lola was not taking aim and her shots went wild and her gun was empty and with no more bullets she threw the gun at me and the gun went flying over my head as I ducked. I reached up and grabbed her by the leg and she fought like a wildcat. The other three didn't know where to go but there was one way down and Chance took it. I pulled Lola down the ladder and got her under control and the wool agent was at the bottom of the ladder with a gun in hand and I took my handcuffs and put them on Lola and left her with the agent and he had taken possession of the money again. I went through the car after Chance. I heard more shooting from above and there was Chance in front of me with a gun in his hand pointing at me. "Get out of my way Jim I want that money. I don't want to shoot you but I will."

"You have to get by me to get it and that won't be easy with an empty gun."

Chance pulled the trigger and it fell on an empty cylinder and I pulled out my gun and walked toward him and there was more shooting from above. Then I glanced to the right and saw a body fall by the window. Chance took a chance and grabbed my gun and it went off right to his chest and he fell in a lump on the floor. That's when Dean came through the door holding his arm and one of the guards in front of him and his gun in his bad arm.

"They creased me it's not bad. You got Lola and the money?"

Lola and the agent were coming from the back of the car.

"The agent has her and the money."

The agent came up to me.

"I see that one didn't make it. I'm James Warren with Smith & Brothers."

We shook hands. "I'm Jim Beddly, Texas Ranger and this is a friend Dean Gibbs."

"Glad to see you two just in time."

"I've been watching them for two days."

Lola spoke up as we pulled into the station. "How could you do this to me Jim?"

"Lola, I warned you and Chance a week ago to stay clean. You seem not to take me at my word."

As we got off the train John and Gary were waiting for us. I saw Red and Dean's horse waiting by the station.

"Why, Jim you are making my job easier you got two more."

"Chance is in that car dead and another is about a mile down the track. He might be dead after that fall."

John led the two away to jail and I turned to Gary.

"Gary, this is James Warren from Chicago."

They shook hands and James said.

"Can I have a beer before we look at the wool."

"Sure thing Mr. Warren. The owner of the Long Bar just went to jail but we'll get you a beer."

"After that ordeal just call me James. Is your man alright?" Dean spoke up.

"I'm fine James just a scratch. Thanks for asking."

After we got in the Long Bar I got James a beer and he just sit there drinking his beer.

"Every time I come out west I really enjoy it. Why would that woman risk losing all this? I sure do like that bar. Well I think I'm ready to get down to business now where's that wool. The train won't wait forever."

We all laughed and James and us headed for the barn. Gary unlocked the lock and I opened the door and James walked in and took a knife out and cut a piece of the end off and pulled some wool out. He smelled it and then felt the wool and rubbed it against his cheek.

"Mighty fine and has a good smell. I can tell that this comes from sheep that were fed well and the touch is of high quality, a sign of good breeding. People think that wool is all the same but it's not."

"Gary, if I may call you Gary."

"You may James."

"I am authorized by my company to pay you twenty thousand more for good quality and this more than meets that. I have a contract here for this year and in it you will find that my company would like you to let us buy from you for the next five year at the market price but I'm changing it to state fifty cents per pound above market price if the wool is of the same quality. I'll be out next year, now have your men get it on the train and we'll go have a beer or two and sign the contract."

"You heard the man get those wagons loaded and on that train. James let's go have that beer."

For five hours we loaded the wool on the train. Gary handed James the contracts and James handed Gary the money as he walked on board the train and the train pulled out of the station. As we were heading back to the ranch all worn out Jerry came running out of the land office. I stopped and the rest of the men went on.

"I saw you here all day, but I was waiting for the last crew to come in. They got it all marked out on every corner. You better ride that land it's more than we thought and the men said so beautiful. They said that there was a kind of road most growd up heading down to one of three water falls. One is near the back portion of the land. Here's the deed and it's all yours all free and clear. I wonder how that place was missed for all these years. You just saved me a long trip out to Gary's."

"Thank you Jerry for all your help."

"They found the other gate on the northeast side. It's marked on the map and it was just as hard to find as the other gate."

I rode Red out of town tired and happy at the same time. I see now I better get in better shape cause my ranch is going to take a lot of work. As I was riding down the dirt trail and thinking a spark of an idea jumped into my mind. The name was going to be "Paradise Valley Ranch". My mind was wondering so much that I was to the ranch before I knew it. I saw Shelly and June on the porch as I rode up.

"Jim, you look as bad as the rest of the men do. You better get cleaned up supper's ready out under the trees." Shelly said.

"I will, we need to talk tomorrow. I'll spend all day with you. I'll take you home later after we eat and I get cleaned up. I want to talk to Tom about something."

"That's fine Jim, I'll be ready."

"June, if you're up to it Shelly and me and I'm sure Dean will come we'll take you home day after tomorrow."

"I'm up to it. If we can used those wagons that Gary has we'll bring back some ore and take it to the assay office."

"You sure."

"Yes, it's been hiding long enough. I think grandpa would want me to enjoy what he found."

I rode along with Shelly all the way to the ranch and I bet I didn't say twenty words. I was thinking of what to say to Tom. We rode up and Tom and Betty came out on the porch.

"Y'all done over there."

"Yes, sir. I didn't know sheep could be such hard work. Tom, can I talk to you alone it's important."

"Sure thing son. Come on over here."

We talked and I said my peace and he said his and he patted me on the back and said.

"I won't say a word. I think you two will be happy."

14

The next morning I showed up early. Shelly was ready, she had already saddled her horse. As we left I saw Tom and Betty standing on the porch looking our way in an embrace. He must have told his wife. We rode for twenty minutes and I stopped in front of the invisible gate of my "Paradise Valley Ranch".

"Shelly lets go in and explore some of this valley. You said you like to explore."

"I do very much but what if someone owns it. They may not like us in there. What if something happens and they can't find us?"

"Nothing's going to happen and we'll leave the gate open. No one would mind us looking around. How could they blame us it's so beautiful?"

"I guess you're right, let's go explore."

"That's a girl."

I reached in the brush and found the rope and pulled it up and tied it off to a large branch so it wouldn't shut on its own. We trotted down the road to where the burned out cabin was. We just sit there and stared at the ruins.

"I would burn everything left so there would be no sign of the evil that went on here."

"How did you know I was thinking along the same lines? Why don't we ride on and see what's up the rest of this road? Then off the road north and south. Haven't you wondered why this valley is so green, not like the area outside of here? Come over this way I'll show you. I found it the first time I was down here."

We rode off the road a ways back pass the pasture and there it was the stream that flows out of the rock. I stopped and got down and helped Shelly down and we walked to where the stream looked like it disappeared into the face of the rock.

"I didn't have time to look where the water came from. I was kind of busy. It looks as though it stops at the rock but we know it doesn't come out on the other side. I've been all over the outside when I was looking for that darn gate."

"It must go underground."

"That's what I think."

I pulled some brush and weeds from in front of the rock and we could see how the water flowed downward like a small waterfall.

"Let's follow it the other way and see where it goes."

We went east or upstream. There were tall cedars and pine trees all along the banks of the stream. Then we came to the end about two miles later and it ended the same way into the face of the rocks.

"You know going south from here towards the area that we first saw this valley there are two more creeks that I know of. We'll have time later to find what else is this way. Let's go to the north."

"Alright, what did you mean we'll have time later?"

"All this isn't going anywhere is it?"

She looked puzzled as we headed north. We passed the road on the east side and the road disappeared into the face of the rock like the west side.

"This must be the other gate. Two ways to get in and a third if you count the way I first came down outside of town. I sure don't recommend that way. Steep as all get out."

We came to an uphill incline of about twenty feet not too steep for a wagon or buggy. As we reached the top there was a flat area of about two hundred feet by three hundred feet. As we looked out over the valley you could see every direction. Looking pass the trees to the north we could see two small waterfall that fell fifty feet.

"Look Shelly there is water to the north. There looks to be meadows in between here and that water source. May be good for cattle or sheep or both. There seems to be room for anything you would want. What do you think of this place now?"

"It's beautiful and from here you can see most of the valley."

"Yea, and it wouldn't be much trouble to put in a road from that main road that cuts across the valley to here. This incline isn't bad for a buggy or wagon and where the burned out cabin is a barn could be put there for the south pastures."

"What's going on Jim? I haven't ever seen you this excited since this may belong to someone else. We better get out of here."

"Shelly, it's hard for me, I don't know the right way to say this. But I'm asking if you--- would you like your house built right here on this spot."

"Now I am confused. Did you just ask me to marry you?"

"Yes, I did. Will you marry me and this will all be ours."

"How do you know this will be ours?"

"I filed on it five days ago and they finished the survey yesterday and I got the deed right here in my vest. They had to survey it cause no one has ever owned this valley."

"I love this, but how about you being a Ranger? You love it."

"I know, but I love you more and I can tell Cap that if he needs me bad at times he can count on me to come running. I have been a Ranger for twelve years helping other people. I think it's time for me to start a life with the woman I love and this place is ours. We can start a family here to be theirs forever. All you have to say is yes. I put the deed in the name of Mr. And Mrs. Jim Beddly."

"Dad did act strange this morning. I'd say yes Mr. Jim Beddly and I have loved you ever since I saw you after I shot at you and I love this valley."

I took her in my arms and kissed her on the very spot our house was going to be built. We stood there and I pointed out where I planned to build things to make this valley a ranch we could be proud of.

"I hope you don't mind but a name came in my mind yesterday."

"What!"

"Paradise Valley Ranch".

"I just love it Jim, I can't wait to start on the house."

"I can start on it and it will be finished by the time we get married. I can buy some cattle from Tom and some sheep from Gary. We can go to Alpine and you can pick out a ring at Todd's general store."

"Oh, Jim a ring. You really do like those sheep."

"Yes a ring and I do like the sheep. You should see the money Gary made off that wool and you don't have to sell the animals and the dogs are wonderful they do most of the work."

"We better get back and tell everyone. I can't wait. I love you and to think that five weeks ago I didn't know this place existed and now it's ours."

"We can even raise some horses."

We headed back to Tom's ranch and told Shelly's parents and her mother cried and Tom was grinning from ear to ear. When Tom heard about the valley being ours he could hardly contain himself. I told him some of the plans and that we found the perfect spot for the house. As we left on the way to Gary's ranch Shelly said.

"You know Jim, Stella's boy doesn't have a name yet."

"I know I've been thinking on that but can't come up with a name. Have you?'

"I've been thinking but it was just a thought but now that we are going to be married. You know I brought him into this world almost like his mother."

"Are you saying what I think your saying?"

"Yes, Jim I want that boy. We can call him J. J. for Jim Jr."

"I never thought of that. That is a catchy name J. J. Beddly. Let's do it we'll talk to Bonnie and Gary."

"Bonnie already knows I want him and I hoped you would ask me to marry you."

"You little devil, you had this all planned."

"Not exactly. Don't be mad."

I laughed. "I'm not mad. All this time I've been so nervous about asking you. Tomorrow Dean and me are taking June over to Marfa to get some ore samples. You want to come."

"You bet I do."

We got to Gary's and Bonnie saw the smile on both of our faces. "He done did it, didn't he?"

"He did."

"Did what? You know what she's talking about, Dean?" Gary said.

"Don't look at me."

Bonnie let out. "You two men, Jim asked Shelly to marry him. Anyone can see that on their faces."

I saw the look in Dean's eyes as he looked over at June.

"Gary, Jim filed on that valley and got it. It's ours and he wants to buy some sheep from you later."

"Glad to hear that. No sense in messing that pretty valley with some old cows. No offence Shelly."

"None taken cause there's enough room for cattle and horses too."

"We have time to go and look it over one day."

"Bonnie, I talked to Jim and we want to take J. J. to be ours."

"What's J. J.?" Dean said.

"His name, Jim Jr."

"That's a handle all right short and sweet." Gary said.

I said, "Gary, tomorrow can we borrow two wagons and Pickin's to drive one and I'll drive the other. We're takin' June to Marfa and get some of that ore and she's going to start mining operations over there. Right June."

"Yes, but I'm going to need someone to help me manager the mine."

"Why you have Dean he's a fast learner."

Gary spoke up. "Why you taking all my men?"

"Oh, Gary you have enough men till shearing season again. Tim is worth two men." Bonnie said.

"That's true he is good."

"I'm taken Shelly home and come back and get ready for tomorrow."

There was a beginning of a road between Gary and Tom's ranch now that the two had become friends. I had supper with the Davis's that night and Shelly and me sat and talked about the future. After we told Tom and Betty about our decision to adopt J. J. they just sat there on the front porch swing and listen to us talk with smiles on their faces. Then Tom said, "Me a grandpa."

"Why Tom don't forget I'll be a grandma." She looked over at us and continued, "And maybe some more babies later. I always wanted to be a grandma."

"Ma, don't rush us we're not married yet." They all were laughing into the night.

The next morning Shelly showed up early cause it was a ways to Marfa and with the wagons we would have to spend a night on the trail maybe two. We had to take enough food for five people and pots and pans. Shelly and me were in one wagon and Pickin's was driving the other wagon we had our horses tied behind and then Dean was driving June in the buggy. She was still getting better but hurt some and the buggy made it a little easier on her. Dean was in the lead and knew where all the waterholes were. The first night we spent at the third water hole. We didn't expect trouble so we had a fire with some good cooking by Shelly and June. Pickin's I could see was enjoying his leisure time in the wagon all day. The days were still hot in these September days but the nights were getting near cold come morning.

The next day was some of the same. By noon we stopped and ate at the last water hole before Marfa. At supper we were about five miles outside of town so we decided to take our time and stay where we were for the night and roll into Marfa in the morning. Our water barrels were half full and there was plenty of water in Marfa. We would spend the next two or three nights in the hotel. We didn't know how long it would take to load the ore. We were sitting around the campfire and June told us.

"I hope there's enough gold to get a good start on the mine. If we have enough to buy some proper mining equipment that will make it easier on the men when we hire some."

"Listen to her Dean already talking like a big shot mining executive."

"Oh, Jim quit teasing me. I just want the town to come back to life. It was grandpa's dream."

"I know June I'm just trying to keep everyone's spirit up."

"I've been so busy this week trying to get better I forgot to thank you for all you did for me and this town."

"That's my job little lady and if it hadn't been for you contacting the Rangers I never would have met this beauty of a lady and you and my best friend Dean. You are going to be my best man."

"Who me?"

"Why sure you, who else would I pick."

"I'm honored. Thank you."

"June will be my maid of honor. Why we've been friends since we were young."

"Thank you Shelly I'll try to serve you well."

We went to bed Shelly and June in the wagon and Pickin's, Dean and me under the wagon. The next morning the girls out did their selves with a breakfast out of this world. We were on the move again and by noon we were coming down Main Street but something was wrong. There were wagons in front of stores and I saw Doby, the bartender in Alpine, going in the saloon. There was Todd in the general store and Jeb in the lively. We pulled up in front of the livery and Jeb came out.

"What's going on here, Jeb?" I said.

"We got together and decided that with the mine will come people and they will need things to live on so we came over to see what we will need over here. Most of us will have two places one here and one in Alpine."

Todd and Maggie came over and Todd helped June down from the buggy.

"We came to repair and clean the buildings but there was no need. Since Sid died I decided to open two banks along with the general store. I think after the mine gets started the railroad will make a spur line over here just for your ore."

"How did you know about the gold?"

"That was I."

We looked around and John was standing there looking so smart.

"Jim told me about the case and I remembered about Guy telling people about the gold mine he found and I figured that all those crooks weren't after no donuts. I just put two and two together and here we are and Jim you gave me a lot of hints." John laughed.

That night we spent in the hotel and the next morning June took us down through the livery to the secret passage down to her house. She took us up into the bedroom where we found her tied up and beaten. She went to the bed and said.

"Come here Jim. Grandpa thought of this. Pull down on that right bedpost at the head of the bed."

I pull the bedpost down and the foot of the bed started to rise to be straight up to the head.

"Shelly, bring that lantern over here and look down in the dark under the bed."

The light showed us a stairway going down and June went first and we all followed. June lit the lanterns, that were hanging on the walls, every fifteen feet or so and the whole tunnel was lit up as we headed north. We came to a huge room that was filled with ore that sparkled in our eyes. Then over on the other side was a room with piles of sacks.

"I did the room with the raw ore and grandpa knew how to separate the gold from the rock. He never got around to showing me before he died. That room with the bags is pure gold. I think we should take the ore and see what it essay out at and maybe some of the pure sacks of gold for the machinery to get started. What do you think Jim or you Dean?"

We were all standing there with our mouths open just staring at the two rooms.

"Jim, Dean, Shelly how about you Pickin's? One of you say something what's wrong?"

I finally got my mind working and my tongue untied.

"June, I never thought you had found anything like this."

"This is just the start the mine is a half mile down that tunnel. The entrance is about a hundred feet down that tunnel that's where I keep the mules to bring the ore from the mine. Dean, you and Pickin's can bring the wagons over to the east about a hundred yards behind the hotel. There are some boulders with a passage in between two of them. You won't see the entrance at first but you'll find it."

Shelly said, "You mean this was right below where Mary and Jimmy had you tied."

"Yes ma'am, grandpa was right smart."

Dean and Pickin's went back out and June took us to the entrance and we were going uphill all the way.

"No wonder I never could find you that first day after you saved my life." I said

"What are you talking about Jim?" Shelly said with a look of concern written all over her face.

"I'll tell you later we have our whole life ahead of us."

It took us two whole days to get the two wagons loaded and Pickin's looked as if he wished he hadn't come with us. June closed up all the tunnels entrances and we pulled the wagons into Main Street and the people gather around the wagon and June spoke to the crowd. "Thank y'all, with your help this will be "The Town That Wouldn't Die"."

Todd spoke as the two wagons started pulling out of town.

"Maggie, I think we ought to get back to town with these wagons. We're the only bank that these two towns have now."

As most that came were now leaving town when Todd and Maggie's buggy came along side June's buggy and Maggie spoke to June.

"You know June, we are just starting up the bank in town and for what I see here we won't have enough money on hand. You'll have credit to buy what you need up to the amount that Eagar come up with. So we are going to go ahead and make contact with a few major banks to start letting banks know there's a big strike here and we will need funds. It will get done and we'll let Eagar know you are coming in and Egar will know where and how to get this pure gold and the ore to where it needs to go."

Jim turned to Dean and June. "We'll have him weigh the bags that Guy separated and that should let you get that equipment faster." Dean said.

"This is the start of something big June. Let's get to town."

It took all of three days to get back to Alpine. The people that left with us were already along the street yelling as we pulled down the main street and stopped in front of the assay office and there coming down the front steps was Eagar with a big smile on his face.

"Hello, been waiting for you to pull in since Todd told me what was coming. I'm all set up inside, get the bags in first and we'll get them weighed out and get them to the bank then I'll start on the ore and see how much to the ton."

We started unloading the wagon and Eagar started weighing. So as he finished we loaded it back in the wagon. When Eagar was done with the full bags he did some figuring and handed June a form with the first total on it. June had a look on her face that I had never seen and she seemed to have some trouble breathing. Dean and me rushed to her. Dean asked.

"You alright June. You hurting again? You want to set down?" She got out,

"No, look at this." She handed the form to Shelly as she came up to help. That did no good as Shelly looked at what June had seen she just had a blank stare on her face so I took it from Shelly's hand and had me a look and I had never heard of this amount before.

"This right Eagar?"

"Sure is. $405,000 and I'll start on the ore now."

Dean helped June and I helped Shelly to the wagon and we got it to the bank where Todd and Maggie were waiting out front. As we helped the women down they were back to normal more or less Maggie spoke as I handed her the form and she stumbled as she looked so Todd took the form and looked.

"We have no room so leave it in the wagon for now. We'll have to ship it out in a few days to Dallas where the bank will send this huge amount to us. It will take awhile but you've been waiting all these years." Todd spoke to this.

"We'll send a telegram to anyone that you might want to get things rolling that we guarantee anything up to this amount and tell them it will be coming in for the foreseeable future. While y'all were heading this way I found some mining equipment companies and I got replies from two and they will be sending a man from each company and they will look things over and let you know what you need at the start."

We saw John walking up as we were talking to Todd.

"I heard what you were saying. Jim, why don't we pull the wagons in the stable and we'll guard this for a few days while Eagar arranges for it to be shipped out."

"Sound's good. Now Todd after we get this in the barn and get the horses settled we would like to see you in your store if that is possible."

Shelly looked at me and I looked at her and a smile came across her face as I was already smiling and she fling her arms around my neck as we were about to climb on the wagon.

"I'll head that way in about twenty minutes. See you two there."

Jeb offered to take care of the horses so we headed to the store with June and Dean along side us. We walked up to the counter when Todd asked,

"Now what can I do for you two?" Shelly spoke up before I could.

"We would like to see your engagement and wedding rings if you don't mind. Isn't that right Jim." Shelly had that big smile and was holding on to my arm.

"Sure as rain."

"Well I'll be. Now that's news."

"Just happened a few days ago."

"Congratulations and here they are in this locked case and I got the key right here."

Todd took out two trays of rings one engagement and one wedding rings. Shelly

picked up one from each tray and tried them on. After three tries she found two that fixed just right on her little fingers.

"These will do just fine. Now you pick your wedding band Jim."

Todd put those two trays away and bought out a tray of men's rings. I tried on two different ones and found just the right one and I looked at Shelly and she knotted her head with that smile still on her face. I told Todd.

"That's it, Shelly you wear the engagement ring and if you have a box for the wedding ring. That will do it."

I heard some noise behind us and Shelly and me turned just as Dean went down on one knee and took June's hand in his and Shelly put her hand to her face.

"June, the first time I saw you I knew you was for me. I know we haven't known each long but that feeling is still with me. I love you. Will you marry me."

June was now crying as she looked down at Dean. Then a smile broke out on her face as she spoke to Dean.

"I had that same feeling and I will marry you. And I do love you so much." Todd said.

"Well I'll be. I'll get the trays back out."

They picked out theirs and the wedding rings were in two boxes as June asked.

"Todd, can I open an account with you. I'm paying for all the rings." Shelly spoke up.

"You can't."

"Yes I can and just say it's Dean and my wedding present to you two. Now Todd do I."

"You sure do and the amount is $243 even."

We left to go to Tom and Betty's ranch. As we rode along the women started to talk and the men just listened at what was being said.

"You know June, don't you think we should get married on the same day? Why you and Dean with be living in Mafia getting that town going along with all the work in the mine so if you were married that would put the temptation away and you could live your life together in peace."

"That would be nice but how soon are you thinking."

"I was thinking Saturday after next."

This is when I spoke up as I looked at Dean.

"Now Shelly, I was going to build our house in that spot we picked out before we wed."

"I know but this way we can move onto our land and work together like the old days of the pioneer."

"In a tent or a cover wagon and carry water from the stream and it might take onto a year."

"I don't think so. We have a lot of friends like my father and his men then there is Gary and Bonnie and his men."

"You think they might. We could get it roughed out in about two weeks and then live in the house while we work on the inside. We can ask and then we could have the wedding Saturday after next. You have anything to say Dean."

"Just that Gary's going to be awful mad for taken more of his men away. But I like the idea of working in the mine and coming home to my wife at night."

"Dean, I have worked in that mine for years so I'll be there all day beside you."

They all had a laugh as the women rode on and talked about more wedding plans. I had on my mind something else completely different. I asked Dean.

"You remember when Joe was killed in the jail?"

"I do and you told me he did say something and you would tell me later."

"Well now is later. Its been worrying on my mind lately. Joe told me Bart told him the boss had a deep scar on the back of his neck under the collar and the gun had been put in his hand. Gave me no name only that."

"I can see why that would worry you with all that gold in town. The undertaker never said anything. We could ask him to be sure."

"You have a good point. After dinner why don't you and I get to town and see who John has guarding that gold and then talk to James in the morning. You know that gold mine will be half yours Saturday after next."

"Now don't you start that."

We were laughing as we rode up to the porch along side the women and there was Tom and Betty standing staring at us.

"What are you four doing and why are you boys laughing?" Tom asked.

"Just having some fun with Dean here about marrying into money." He poked me and I laughed again. Shelly said, looking at me with a frown.

"Us women had a more serious talk. We all decided to get married on the same day Saturday after next." Betty said to the girls.

"That is so soon and June, you and Dean are getting married." She was saying as we dismounted.

"Yes ma'am. He asked me in the store when Shelly was getting their rings so we are in love and decided to get married to. Anyway we'll be working together in Mafia for a long time." They showed Betty their rings as they talked.

"Well let's get inside and eat to y'all marriage."

After dinner Dean and me were on the road to town. It was toward sundown as we came in a back way into town. We didn't want to be seen right away. We stopped and watched as John came out of his office and headed home hopeful for the night. I said to Dean.

"We just saw John go in his house. I just wonder who's watching the gold."

"I'll go down with my horse and put it in a stall and see. Don't worry I have a reason set in my mind."

Dean went across the street and went in the stable and I was worried but he came out in about ten minutes.

"Well what happen?"

"He hired Jeb to watch the wagon tonight and he said John told him you would be in tomorrow night and me the next night and John would watch it the fourth night before the banks men get here the next afternoon and leave the morning after that. Told him we thought I was on duty tonight but I would drink a beer and get a room in the hotel. Not any since getting on that road in the dark with no moon out."

We stayed on to watch all night and in the morning I made my way down the street to the undertaker as Dean came up with his horse ready to go. We walked in and James was there at his desk. James asked,

"What y'all two doing in town this early. I thought Bonnie made a fine breakfast."

"She does and it was great about an hour ago. But we wanted to talk to you and then go see John about tonight at the barn, June has a lot riding on that. Could you tell me if one of the men we brought in had a deep scar on their neck just under the collar."

"No, can't say I saw anything like that. Only scar was Bart on his face and we all knew about that. Believe it or not Mary had a tattoo on her butt cheek of an Angel."

"Fine, thanks." As we walked out of the undertaker we saw John but he didn't see us.

15

John was leading his horse to the stable and it was loaded with a big pack on its back. He went in and came out in twenty minutes. We went to his office and went in. He looked up at us then I asked.

"I'm coming in tonight to watch the gold and Dean will be in tomorrow."

"That's right and I'll take the last night before the men come to pick up the gold the next afternoon. I'm going along with them for a day or two then be back. They should be fine after that."

"I guess that will help make anyone think twice with another man along and a lawman at that. I assume they will be back with wagons for the ore."

"That seems reasonable. See you later this evening."

We left and tied our horses in front of the Long Bar and went in for a beer. I told Dean,

"You go back to the ranch this stinks to high heaven. Something's not right. I was sure the guards were going to take the gold back by train and Johns talking about following it for two days."

Dobie placed two glasses of beer on the bar and I looked around and asked.

"Dobie, who owns the bar now." He looked and smiled at me.

"Why I do. Todd is looking through the bank records but hasn't found anything yet at least till Lola gets out of prison." And the smile disappeared.

"I hope you get to keep it. Just keep it honest." He smiled,

"Oh, I intend to saw what happened to the other owners."

We finished our beers and Dean headed to the ranch and it was almost sundown so I headed to the stable with Red behind me. I unsaddled Red and got him some hay and oats and handed Jeb five dollars and walked over to check the gold. It was there cause I had counted the number of sacks and they were all present. It was going to be a long night but June was counting on this gold. I looked around the barn area then out in the corral everything was normal as I could see but it crossed my mind why did Jeb have three mules in there. I went inside and settled down near the wagons just to keep a close eye on anything that might happen but all was quiet when Jeb started to leave. That's when I asked him.

"When did you start handling mules I thought they had to be ordered special?"

"They sure do and John had me get them about two weeks ago and they just came in this morning. They cost a pretty penny to."

"Did he say why he wanted mules?"

"Just said might have to follow the gold to Dallas. Said he might take his wife for a good time in the big city."

"She has a horse or were they going to take a buggy, be more comfortable for her."

"You know I thought that and I asked and you know what he said."

"No, what?"

"Said she can ride great and loves to ride. But I'm thinking that's a far piece and could be hard on a woman's backside if not use to it. Well, I better get home before the wife comes looking for me."

I had to think about this so I set my back to the wheel of the wagon and had me a think as I often do when alone and I sure was going to be alone except of the livestock. Now John didn't know to much about the gold two weeks ago. Did he make a mistake about following the gold when I was sure it was going by train and it was already loaded on wagons. Why would they come back for the ore with more wagons. I sure wasn't going to ask John anything about this, just let it play out and see what happens. I hope he's not turned bad. In my thoughts the night went by fast and Jeb was at work and I left for the ranch. I didn't think someone would try for the gold in the bright sunshine with Jeb there all day and I missed Shelly some bad.

As I rode up to the porch there was Shelly and June watching shading their eyes from the morning sun and the smell of eggs and pancakes was in the air.

"Come on in for breakfast it's on the table."

"Sounds mighty good, my stomach was about to crawl away from me."

I kissed Shelly as we headed inside and sat with Tom just awaiting with Betty then Tom asked as we sat down and the cakes were passed around the table.

"How'd it go last night I heard June fidgeting all night long."

"I know she was right next to me." Shelly said as we started to eat.

"I can't help it with that gold in that old barn and me out here. Just been so use to hiding and no one around. Just hard." I took June's hand in mine as tears started to wield up.

"Don't worry Dean will be there tonight and John tomorrow night. No matter what happens it will get to Dallas and I'll make sure of that." The tears dried up as we finished.

"I better get and shoo Dean to town for a long night and me I'm going to sleep most the day. Those critters in the stable sure kept me awake all night especially this one."

I patted Red on the neck as I mounted and headed to Gary's of course after I bent out of my saddle to kiss Shelly.

"I'll check in on J. J. before I lay down." I yelled as I turned to leave.

"Tell Bonnie I'll be over later today to take care of him. We get to take him home after the wedding."

Dean had not a bit of trouble this night except trying to stay awake. The last night before the guards were coming from the bank in Dallas John was on guard duty but I was not to sure about him now. My insides just were feeling like something was wrong and that feeling stayed with me most of the night but I did finally fall asleep for the last three hours before Dean and Pickin' shook me awake. I was startled as I jumped up and got dressed fast and they just looked at me as I told Dean.

"Come on we need to hurry to town."

"Before we eat?"

"I'll saddle the horses and you grab something to eat. We'll eat it on the way. Tell Bonnie, it has to do with the gold. She'll understand. Now get."

On the way to town I explained to Dean what I was thinking and he had a puzzled look on his face.

"You think John was mixed up in this all along."

"If the gold is there no but if not and he's gone then yes. He thinks so much of Paula that I think he'll do almost anything for her happiness."

We were coming into the main street fast enough to make the dust rise into the still air of the town and pulled to a stop in front of the stable with a flying leap off Red, I fling open the stable doors as I saw Jeb come running up from down the street.

"What's going on Jim?"

"Don't know for sure yet." I rushed to the stalls and looked over at the wagons. They were there but John and Paula's horses were gone.

"Jeb, look out back for the mules." I said as Dean and me ran to the wagons, I pulled back the tarp on the wagon with the full gold pouches and they were gone every last one of them. Jeb was running back in the back door of the stable yelling.

"Jim, the mules are gone and no sign of John. He was here when I went home at seven last night, acted kind of fidgety and I asked what was wrong and he said he was glad when the gold was out of town."

"I'll check John's office and Dean; you go get Tim and get Bonnie to put together food and have Tim track my horse and the mules are plain in sight. Look over here the tracks lead toward our ranch. I'll be gone."

I left for the sheriff's office, no John which I expected but on the wall where the rifles were kept they were all gone and looked to be a fast pull out and the photograph on the wall was gone of John or should I say Tim Dolan. As I was leaving Eagar came through the door.

"What's going on Jim?"

"Looks like John took off with the bagged gold. If we aren't back by the time the train gets in tell the men from the bank in Dallas to take the raw ore on and we'll get the other to them when we get back."

"I'll get it done."

I took off on Red and we were out of town following all the tracks of five animals, two horses and three mules. He sure wasn't trying to hide where he was going and it led right up to the hide-a-way gate on my ranch that we had just bought. I don't know what he was thinking but I knew of no other way out but the other two that I had found but I hadn't been much to the north of the ranch. I kept following the tracks and they stopped right at the edge of the stream that came from one of the waterfalls. I went along one bank and then the other and no tracks came out of the water. Now I was puzzled as I walked looking all around leading Red. I stopped and thought as I headed back to the open gate. I thought he might have back tracked but outside the gate was no other recent tracks except the ones I had followed from town. I was at a dead end, I had to wait for Tim.

Tim and Dean showed up in about an hour and they were leading three saddled horses behind them. Tim got out of the saddle fast and was looking at the ground starting to walk toward where I had been by the stream and he told me.

"Brought more horses when ours tire we use these and lead ours. We have not so tired horses as they will. Will slow them down and we catch." He walked right up to the stream all the way to the waterfall, as I had done. He moved closer to the waterfall and to our amazement he walked right through the water falling all around him. He came back through dripping wet and led his two horses to the other side of the stream. He told us,

"Go all the way through behind falls. Can see light not too far, come."

Dean and me looked at each other and followed Tim as he went on another hundred feet and then mounted on the outside where it turned dry looking again. I couldn't help but say.

"I wonder where the water comes from to make those falls and that's another secret entrance. Look how dry it is on this side."

Tim led the way as I now could see the tracks of the mules as we went on. Tim said after an hour.

"Five hours ahead no more. Switch horses let ours rest now."

We stopped by a small stream to let the horses water and rest as we fixed coffee and heated some food that Bonnie had sent.

"That means they could be in Fort Stockton already. They're heading in that direction for now."

"Looks to me going that way but I have not been all the way to this Fort Stockton. Was told was wanted this far east, so never go."

"You just follow their trail in case they try to pull a trick on us and I'll deal with the people in the towns we come to." Dean said to us as we headed east.

"You know you have a wedding to attend to come next Saturday. You didn't even tell Shelly we were going. She might think you left the country and not coming back." He laughed as we kept moving at a faster pace on the extra horses and lead our horses behind.

"You're real funny. I'm sure Bonnie or Gary will fill her in on what happened. By the way I don't seem to remember you telling June why or when we left." It was my turn to laugh and Tim let out a little snicker.

"Lord almighty, I plum forgot I am getting married that same day. Tim, let's get a move on." Tim and me really laughed out loud at Dean as he became very serious and tried to rush Tim along.

We had been on the trail almost five hours when we saw signs of more traffic and a town up ahead.

"We'll stop in at the Sheriffs office, his name is Jeff Huff if I remember."

We stopped in front of the Sheriffs and Jeff was right out front when we rode up.

"Why hello there Jim been a long time. I see you still are wearing that badge."

As we let the horses water in the trough I told Jeff.

"Might say the same for you."

"Yea, seems we both can't get away from the law." He laughed then continued.

"Knowing you I know you didn't stop in just to jaw with me. Must be that man and woman with three mules trailing behind."

"You're right on target as always. Don't have much time if you have any information."

"Sure was wondering about those two but he showed Mr. Becker at the bank his badge. Mr. Becker told me later John wanted to get paper money for the gold but Becker didn't have enough. Said they were on their way to San Antonio to catch a train to the east. That's all I know except that was six hours ago."

"Thanks, this is my partner Dean and this is Tim our tracker a very good friend. We better get on their trail."

We left Jeff standing on the porch and were out aways when Tim said.

"Not go straight east more north. Easy to follow. We go this way."

"That goes toward Abilene and then Ft. Worth. That's a far piece."

The trail kept to the same direction so we took a chance and went on into the night. We ate in the saddle some of the cold biscuits and jerky that were tasty put together sort of but not like cooking over an open fire. About midnight we stopped but were to tired to cook so we curled up and was asleep and up and on the trail by four before any sign of the sun but we had a few hours of a full moon that had us following the mules tracks. By ten in the morning the heat was on us like an oven set to cook a meal. By four in the afternoon we were riding up the streets of Abilene and there was the Sheriffs office so we rode up as our horses were about worn out. As we dismounted we tied the horses right in front of the horse trough, all six of them. The Sheriff came out and I shook his hand. He said.

"I'm Dave Cott. I see you're a Texas Ranger. What may I do for you?"

"Looking for a man and woman with three mules tagging along behind. He was the Sheriff in Alpine but what's on those mules makes him an outright thief. I'm Jim Beddly." I shook his hand.

"I seen those two but he stopped in to talk to me and said there was a man following him that claims to be a Texas Ranger. Said he use to be but took a more in one place job to have a life said his name was Tim Dolan now the Sheriff of Alpine. He was transporting what was on the mules to Dallas and taking his wife for a little fun in the big city."

"I'll tell you that is gold and it should have been on the train two days ago but he lit out with it and that is his true name and I use to ride with him in a Ranger outfit. He quit and changed his name to John Brady and became the Sheriff of Alpine, just got a little greedy and there were four murders there. Haven't linked him to them but he was involved someway. If you have a telegraph you can contact my Captain John Turbrough."

He smiled and looked the way of the livery and said after pulling a piece of paper out of his pocket.

"No need I already sent one and the reply is right here. Thought it funny he had his wife with him and I've known Cap John for years been here many times. Just had a feeling you would show up cause John let me know your name and you was on leave but guessed you found out more. Said you were that kind of man. Your man is in the saloon and his wife is in the hotel, guess he thought he outran you and your men, the mules are in the livery. Even tried to turn the gold into currency, the banker came to me said no way he would take a chance like that. Thought it stolen and so did I. I had a deputy looking after the mules since I got this gram back." I smiled.

"I better get a long to the saloon. Dean, you ready. Tim, you can go look after the mules let the deputy get back to work." Dean told us.

"Ready boss, we have a wedding to get to."

"I go with you; you help me and family. Make sure you alright." Cott put in with a smile.

"I like that, loyal men. My deputy will be alright where he is. You need any help; the jail is available if need be."

"Thanks, but I think we can handle what comes."

We walked off the porch and down the dusty street like I have a dozen times in the past except this time I had some good friends to back me up. I knew that Tim Dolan was fast on the draw from his reputation as a Texas Ranger. As we kept walking to the saloon I said.

"You two don't get involved between Tim Dolan and me. Just keep an eye open for men that have gone to his side. You never know what brand of men are in the saloon."

There was loud music coming out of the saloon as we stepped up on the porch and pushed open the bat-winged door as hard as I could, so there would be no doubt that I had come on business. All eyes turned our way except for one pair and Tim turned around slow and had a big smile on his face, a smile that I had never seen, that said all that needed said. He spoke right out to the whole crowd.

"Boys, this is Jim Beddly a fine Texas Ranger and till recently a good friend along with the other two but things have changed a little since the old days. Now Jim come have a drink on me I can afford it now." He laughed and I spoke out.

"Tim, you are under arrest for murder and robbery. You others, I don't know but my men here will take care of any of you that want to buy into our business. Come on Tim I have a jail cell ready for you. I'll make sure Paula is taken care of."

He just laughed again and downed the rest of his drink and slammed the glass down hard on the bar breaking it to bits. As the glass broke the two men moved away from Tim that left him all alone as his eyes blinked and he started to draw as the other two had to his right and left. I heard two guns go off in my ears as I fired and all three men in front of us laid dead on the floor. I just looked down at Tim and shook my head as I bent down and pulled down his collar then I looked to my left and right and smiled and said.

"See Dean I told you; you were faster than me and Tim, I am very surprised at you."

"I had to be fast the way men were always on my trail." Then Dean spoke up as Dave came through the doors.

"That's still in debate but I'm on your side so it doesn't really matter. Does it?"

"No it don't." Cott spoke out.

"I see you won't be needing my jail after all. Boys take these bodies to the undertaker. What you going to do now Jim?"

"It's to far to take it back to Alpine so I guess we're going on to Dallas. How far is it Dave?"

"May be a day pullin' those lunk-headed mules but if I was you and I'm not I would get over to the train station before it pulls out and you might get there before the bank closes."

"You heard him, lets get going. Here Cott is two hundred dollars for Paula Tim's wife. If I remember right she has kin somewhere in Arkansas this should get her there and some extra."

Dean and Tim went to the stable and paid the bill for the mules as I went to buy a place in one of the stock cars and we would be riding with the stock. We were loading the stock as the whistle blew to leave, we were inside and the train crew was closing the door to the rail car. We laid down in the hay that was on board and Dean tucked his hands back under his head with a piece of straw hanging out his mouth.

"Might not be a bad ride. Just six hours and we'll be there. I'm just going to take a nap."

"You can but we still have this gold to watch over. Don't mean someone don't have something planned before there."

"I just don't see it that way. How about you Tim?"

"Me know a lot of men were in saloon and he must said something to the men there or those two would not have backed him."

"See Dean, just what I been thinkin', just not out loud."

"Y'all two wake me if anyone drops in."

The train was moving along nice and steady down the track as noon came and went. We had the door open looking at the landscape pass by when I heard a sound coming from on top of the car. I motioned to Tim to go up the ladder on the north end and I went up the ladder on the south end. We both poked our heads out as we opened the lid over the hole on top with our guns drawn and looked every which way but nothing. We moved back down and tried to relax but for me it was impossible. Dean was still snoring away as more sounds came to us. Red started moving around and snorting as a shoot rang out from the open door. We ducked and saw two riders come into view. They had been at the wrong angle to hit us. They started dropping back and we ran to the door as Dean came fast to his feet. I carefully looked and saw two men leave their saddles for ladders at the end of the car two cars back. I shut the door and all three of us headed for the ladders. As we reached the top and looked out there were two men coming from each direction. Two must have been in the passenger car that we heard before waiting for the ones on horseback. Lead started flying at us as we jumped down the ladders after putting a bar through the latch on the hatch. We got the horses to the other side of the car just as more lead rained down. We opened the door again and Dean and me saw a small track that the doors rode on all the way to near the ladders on each end.

"Tim, stay in here and keep a gun on those hatches and shoot to kill if they make it through."

Dean and me made our way along the tracks and barely holding on to the side of the car. The shooting had stopped as we made the ladders and started up as we reached the top and looked over we saw four men shooting into the roof of the car again. I yelled.

"You're under arrest put up your hands."

They started shooting my way as I ducked down below the rim of the car. This left Dean a clear target from behind them. Dean was firing and hit one in the leg and another one in the arm and their guns were dropped on the roof. I looked over the rim and the other two were looking from where I was to where Dean was and took a flying leap over the side of the car just as we passed a river. We watched as they landed in the water but didn't see them come up from under the water, the train was just moving to fast. We yelled at Tim and he opened the hatches and we got the two wounded down the ladders. They wouldn't speak a word as we pulled into the Dallas train station at three in the afternoon. We got our horses and mules with the gold packed on top unloaded and a porter pointed us toward the Sheriff's office. As we walked in with the two wounded men tied up I told the Sheriff after he looked at the badge on the front of my shirt.

"Just might need a little doctor's care. The other two jumped in the river right outside of town. So if you see two damp men walking into town you have your men. I'm Jim Beddly your friendly Texas Ranger. They tried to take the gold off the train that we have outside with my Deputy looking after it and this is Dean Gibbs my other Deputy."

"I guess you're friendly if one don't cause any trouble. I'm Dan Bedlow." They all had a laugh except the two prisoners as they shook hands.

"We need to get to the bank with June Grayson's gold and then this one and me." I patted Dean on the shoulder. "We need to catch the train back to Alpine where we are both getting married in a little over a week." A smile came on Dean's face as he said.

"If they haven't forgotten what we look like in a week."

We made it to the bank and met with the bank president Mr. Becker. As we explained everything that had happen he listened with sincerity and give us a receipt and pass book for June. We went to the train depot to paid for our ride back home with four days to spare before the wedding. The train was leaving at six so I went to the telegraph office and let Cap know all that had happened on my month off and that I was getting married and retiring except if he needed me in an emergency. As the train pulled into the station to slow to a stop we loaded our horses and the three mules with no packs.

We all settled into our seat of the passenger car now that we didn't have any gold to protect. After those days on the trail all three of us fell asleep and I didn't wake up till it was way after midnight and a new day was beginning and a new life for me. Dean and Tim were still silent in the dark of the still moving train as the car swayed back and forth as the night passed. I fell asleep again till the train was slowing and my eyes flung open and the other two were wide awake staring at me.

"Come out of it Jim we're here and we'll get to the ranch. June and Shelly will be waiting to see us. I hope." He laughed and Tim said.

"Can't wait see Little Fawn and children Chico and Blue Deer and sheep."

The town looked the same but it sure was nice to see once more as we unloaded the horses and took the mules and three extra horses to the stable.

As we came to the fork in the road, one towards Gary's and the other to Tom's, Tim said.

"See you at wedding, not want to miss that of my new friends." That said he was gone towards Gary's and we rode to Tom's. The two women must have been looking towards town cause we were barely in sight of the house went two horses were coming our way and there were Shelly and June coming at us bigger than life itself. Not more than a hundred feet between us they jumped off their horses and were running so we came out of the saddles and we all met in the middle with arms flung around each other and lips met in the middle of the trail. It was like we had been gone a year or more instead of just six days. Shelly was the first to speak.

"Thought you were never getting back. Not knowing if you were dead or alive after what we went through in that cabin on our land."

"We should have telegraph you from Dallas when we left the gold at the bank." Dean spoke up as we walked towards the house leading the horses.

"That's right June we got your gold in the bank and here's your pass book."

"I rather have you than all the money."

"Well now darling you got both. How about that Jim? A woman like that." Dean and me laughed as the women just looked at us not even a smile anywhere near their mouth but then burst out in more laughter as we reached the porch where Tom and Betty stood just looking at us wondering what was going on. Tom looked and asked.

"What went on out there on the trail?"

"Tom, we got the gold to Dallas after a shootout in Abilene but it started me thinking when Joe was shot in the jail. He told me that Bart had told him that the main man behind it all had a scar under his collar and none of the people we caught or was killed had that scar and Joe also said the gun was put in his hand and John or I knew he was Tim Dolan a former Texas Ranger was the only one in the room and then he started acting strange. Sure enough after the shootout in Abilene I saw that scar under his collar."

"Who would have known. Bad man always make some kind of mistake. Never expected that of him." Betty spoke out,

"Come on in here and get some supper before it gets cold." Shelly spoke out as we headed in,

"We'll talk about the wedding."

"What about the wedding."

"June and I decided to have it on our property where we are going to build our home."

"Kind of hard to find for the town folk that might want to come." Tom spoke.

"It was but took no time for Gary and my men to clear out that area and build a new gate letting everyone know where the new ranch is."

"Dean, we have to see this. We'll go out tomorrow." The two brides to be spoke up at the same time.

"We're going." Everyone around the table laughed.

The next morning saw us on the way to our ranch all four of us but the surprise I got when we rode up close was never in my mind in a hundred years.

16

The gate had been widen out for enough room so two wagons and a horse in between could pass. There was stone walls on both sides of the path about four feet high and twenty feet down the path. Then over the gate was a sign made out of iron in huge letters that read "Paradise Valley Ranch" and under that "Owners Mr. and Mrs. Jim Beddly". I sat there a while to take it all in.

"Dean, I thought we were gone only about a week. This must had taken a month if not more."

"Looks that way to me and look a regular driveway. Looks to go all the way where you wanted the house." Shelly spoke up as we rode up the drive

"You know with my pa and his men and Gary and his men then ma and Bonnie with June and Sara watching the baby and me bringing dinner all the way out here. You know what sir I even did some of the work on that wall. We got it all done except our home."

"I'll be. You believe that Dean." Dean and me laughed.

"I'm sure impressed."

We rode on and on cause I knew that where the house was to be was bout half a mile into the property. The site where the house was to be was just up the rise as the horses took the climb fine and that drive was going all the way to the top. As we reached the top it could be seen where most everything had been cleared away and was ready for the start of the house. Dean and me dismounted and helped the girls off and I reached into my saddlebag and came out with a book that I had seen in a store in Dallas.

"What's that Jim?"

"Just a little drawing book I found in Dallas and I had enough time to make some drawing of what I thought our home should look like on the train coming back. Here Shelly look and you can change anything or add things that I might have left out."

"I didn't know you were an artist." Shelly said as she turned the pages and studied all the details on every page.

"Just a little hobby I have when I was out on the trail late at night by the flicker of the fire late at night."

"These are great, look June on these back pages are the inside of the house with every room in great detail."

"You need to get started on this as soon as the wedding is over. This can be your honeymoon every night after the men leave." Her and Dean laughed as she continued. "You know Shelly your father will help with his men and Gary. Like an old barn raising. Jim, I have an idea would you draw another house like this maybe a little different for Dean and me. I've been thinking about building a house for us by the new entrance to the mine that going in soon as the equipment comes in. I'll pay you. You did so much for me."

"Nonsense, that was my duty and the drawings will be my wedding gift to the both of you."

"Alright you won't take pay so you buy cattle and sheep from Tom and Gary and that will be our wedding present to you two. Before you say anything, no argument from either of you from the owners of the "Marfa Mining Company"." They all had a great laugh and headed back to the ranch to prepare for the wedding of both couples.

The next three days were like a whirlwind and the morning of the big wedding at the ranch was upon them. The brides were getting gussied up in the house on Tom's ranch and Jim and Dean were getting all decked out in the bunkhouse as all the men were kidding them all in fun of course. As they were saddling their horses Tom showed up and put his hand on Jim's shoulder.

"Jim, I just want you to know how grateful Betty and me are for what you did for us and Gary. You are marrying our only daughter but we are so happy you are the one she picked and you'll be living close by. You just don't know how I feel right now. Shelly told us of the plans for the house on y'all's place so we got together with Gary and Bonnie and we all decided all our wedding gift to you and Shelly will be help building that house so you can really start your life off right. Now you two better get along to your ranch we are starting that way in a few minutes. So get now."

"Tom, I will always try to make Shelly happy and with that big of a ranch give you and Betty lots of grandchildren. I'll need them to run the ranch." He laughed and they mounted and left for their ranch. Looking back to wave, Jim could see Tom rubbing his eyes and Shelly was coming out of the house with June and Betty. He turned quick so not to spoil anything.

As they rode up to the now wide gate it was already open so they moved on and as they came to the incline where the house would be on top they saw buggies and horses all along the road all the way up to the home site. There seemed to be everyone from town there and at the top was all kinds of decoration on most of the trees around the site and there in the center was the preacher standing straight with his Bible in his two strong hands. He waved to us to come forth through all the people standing waiting for the Brides. The people patted us on our backs as we passed with a smile on their faces and a kind word to be said. I saw everyone from the two ranches with Gary and Bonnie on the front row with Sara holding the baby J. J. and as young as he was he looked to have a smile on his face. He would get to see his new parents get hitched. Now everyone turned as a buggy could be heard coming up the drive as Dean and me stood by the preacher. There were the Brides as Tom came to a stop and helped the Brides down and then Betty. Tom looked so proud as he had a Bride on each side of him as they came up the center of the people standing along the way. As they came close the preacher said.

"Who gives away these lovely Brides."

"I do." Tom said and kissed each on the cheek and went to stand by Betty with Gary and Bonnie next to them. The preacher started the ceremony.

"We are gathered here today on this bright and sunny day to unite these two couples until the end of their young life's. Would the couples join right hands. Do you Jim Beddly take Shelly Davis as your wife, to have and hold for better or worst in health or sickness to the day you do part."

"I do."

"Do you Shelly Davis take Jim Beddly for your husband, to have and hold for better or worst in health or sickness to the day you do part."

"I do." Shelly said with a big smile on her beautiful face.

He turned to the other couple and smiled down on them.

"Do you Dean Gibbs take June Grayson to be your wife, to have and hold for better or worst in health or sickness to the day you do part."

"I do." Dean looked like he was going to faint out right but held up as Jim was laughing under his breath, Shelly poked him in the ribs just a little.

"Do you June Grayson take Dean Gibbs to be your husband, to have and hold for better or worst in health or sickness or wealth to the day you do part."

"I do." Dean looked around and someone yelled "Way to go Dean." The preacher just had to add wealth cause everyone now knew about June's gold mine.

"Do the couples have the rings." Dean had Jim's and Jim had Dean's for they were each other's best man. The right rings got in the right hands.

"Please place the rings on the left hand of your Bride. Now do the Brides have the men's rings." June and Shelly gave each other the men's ring and they placed them on the left hand of the two men.

"That done, I now pronounce both of you couples man and wife. You can kiss your own Bride." All laughed and applauded. Then Tom held up his hand to quiet everyone and started.

"We are going to have a party right under those beautiful trees where the tables are and dancing. Everyone might know but if you don't right here is where my daughter and her new husband will build their home and I have the plans right here so Monday we start on it, so anyone that wants to help are welcome. It's going to be an old fashion house raising, with food and drink and a lot of work and I have another set of plans that Jim drew for June and Dean and we'll do the same for them over yonder in "The Town That Wouldn't Die." Have fun today cause Monday the work begins."

The End

Printed in the USA
CPSIA information can be obtained
at www.ICGtesting.com
JSHW021450091124
73282JS00001B/3

9 781778 835308